"Please!" Sarah leapt to her feet. "I don't remember any of that. I don't want to remember!"

"Well, I can't forget, Sarah. You've got a tiny strawberry mark right there." Ben touched her, his fingertips caressing her.

Her flesh burned as though he had branded her, and desire bloomed. "How could you know...?"

"I loved you too much to forget anything about you. And this is what I remember the best."

Before she knew what was happening, Ben had taken her in his arms, his mouth claiming hers in a fierce kiss. She couldn't breathe; she couldn't think. She could only feel. Reckless feelings so staggering she went weak all over, unable to resist the caress of his tongue, the way he crossed and recrossed her mouth with his.

With exquisite familiarity...

Dear Reader,

When winter weather keeps you indoors, what better way to pass the time than curling up with Harlequin American Romance? Warm yourself from the inside out with our very special love stories!

There's something appealing about a big, strong man learning to care for a small child, and Linda Cajio's hero in *Family to Be*, the first book in our brand-new miniseries THE DADDY CLUB, is no exception. Ross Steadwell started The Daddy Club to help other single fathers like him—come see what happens when a woman gets in on the fun!

And what's a man to do when the woman of his dreams gets amnesia—and doesn't remember that he's the father of her child? In Charlotte Maclay's *A Daddy for Becky*, Ben Miller has an innovative answer! And up-and-coming author Darlene Scalera is not to be missed with her tale of a million-dollar marriage offer in *Man in a Million*.

Finally, Debbi Rawlins has concocted a whimsical tale of two sisters who trade places for a week and fall in love with men they wouldn't otherwise have met. *His, Hers and Theirs* offers two special heroines, two sexy heroes, two heartwarming love stories—all in one book!

A whole new year is just beginning—start it off right by treating yourself to our four newest American Romance novels!

Happy New Year!

Melissa Jeglinski
Associate Senior Editor

A Daddy for Becky

CHARLOTTE MACLAY

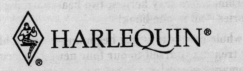

HARLEQUIN®

TORONTO • NEW YORK • LONDON
AMSTERDAM • PARIS • SYDNEY • HAMBURG
STOCKHOLM • ATHENS • TOKYO • MILAN • MADRID
PRAGUE • WARSAW • BUDAPEST • AUCKLAND

ISBN 0-373-16806-3

A DADDY FOR BECKY

Visit us at www.romance.net

Printed in U.S.A.

ABOUT THE AUTHOR

Charlotte Maclay can't resist a happy ending. That's why she's had such fun writing more than twenty titles for Harlequin American Romance and Love & Laughter, plus several Silhouette Romance books as well. Particularly well-known for her volunteer efforts in her hometown of Torrance, California, Charlotte's philosophy is that you should make a difference in your community. She and her husband have two married daughters and two grandchildren, whom they are occasionally allowed to baby-sit. She loves to hear from readers and can be reached at: P.O. Box 505, Torrance, CA 90501.

Books by Charlotte Maclay

HARLEQUIN AMERICAN ROMANCE

Author's Note

I would hope nothing in this book would be construed as disrespect toward the Amish people or their beliefs. The Amish I have met—and those I've researched—indicate most members of the community are deeply devoted to their religion and to their way of life.

This is solely a work of fiction intended for the pleasure of those who love romance and happy endings. Enjoy!

Prologue

Every bone in his body ached, his head throbbed and the smell of antiseptic made him sick to his stomach.

Carefully, Benjamin Miller opened one eye.

A hospital room. White. Sterile. A drab curtain pulled across the end of his bed.

He frowned, trying to remember how he'd gotten there, and his forehead pulled tight. Gingerly he touched his head. A stiff bandage covered a goose egg that was so tender he sucked in a quick breath when his fingers brushed against it.

An accident, he realized. He'd been on his Harley. The bike had hit a patch of ice—

The memory slammed into him with the same force as the telephone pole he'd hit.

"Sarah!" he shouted, sitting up so quickly his head spun, his body violently protesting the sudden movement. Sarah had been on the bike, too, trusting him to keep her safe.

He threw off the covers, swung his legs over the side of the bed, ignoring the IV that was stuck in his arm. He had to find Sarah—the woman he loved more than life itself. And she loved him. They were going to marry—

"Easy does it, Mr. Miller." A nurse hurried into the room in response to the beeping IV machine.

Despite her efforts to hold him down, Ben got to his feet. The room tilted but he stayed upright.

"Sarah…Sarah Lapp. She was on the bike with me. Where is she? Was she hurt? I've got to—"

"You have had a bad concussion, Mr. Miller. Please—"

"No." He shrugged away from the nurse. His head pounded as though a whole army of construction workers had taken up residence inside his skull. "Tell me where—"

"You've been unconscious for three days. It's dangerous for you to—"

He staggered toward the door. "I'm going to find—"

"Your friend is gone."

Ben froze, then whirled unsteadily toward the nurse. "Gone? You mean she's…" He couldn't say the word. Not his beautiful Sarah dead. The girl he'd rescued from ruffians on the streets of Philadelphia six months ago. The woman he loved.

"Her parents took her home. She's recovering there."

His mind was so muddled he had trouble processing that information. Sarah was Amish, or she had been until she had left the community to pursue a nursing education. Leaving meant she was shunned by everyone she'd ever known, including her family. She'd had no contact with them since the day she'd boarded a bus for Philadelphia. Even the letters she'd written had been returned unopened.

He reached for the end of the bed to steady himself. "How did her parents find her?" he asked the nurse.

"She asked that we contact them." The nurse took his arm. "Please, Mr. Miller—"

"Did she leave a message for me? A note? Anything?"

"I'm sorry."

That didn't make sense. Sarah wouldn't leave him. Not without a single word. Maybe her parents had kidnapped her, taken her against her will.

He'd go after her, that's what he'd do. He'd rescue her again if he had to.

His clothes. He needed his...

He turned his head too quickly, searching for a closet, and the room tilted again. His knees started to buckle. He fought the pain, struggled to stay on his feet. But slowly a black curtain descended over his eyes and he crumpled to the floor.

His last thought was of finding Sarah.

THREE DAYS LATER he was released from the hospital. Still battered and unsteady on his feet, he began his search for Sarah. He started looking for her in the Amish community where she'd been raised. But no one would talk to him; no one would tell him where Sarah was.

He expanded his search, spending summer weekends traveling the back roads of Pennsylvania and even going as far as Ohio.

As months passed and then a year, he became discouraged. But he never gave up hoping to find his Sarah again. When he had the time—vacations and scattered weekends—he visited Amish towns, even became friends with merchants in the communities who were not themselves Amish but had business dealings with them. He didn't want to accept defeat but his search became sporadic.

Still, whenever he rode into an Amish town or walked through the business district, Ben always searched the crowd for a familiar face. For Sarah.

It had been six years now. Six years and still he couldn't find her.

Then one day the miracle happened. He spotted his Sarah.

Chapter One

"Sarah! Wait! It's me, Ben."

She glanced back over her shoulder. For a moment their eyes met—hers the same deep shade of blue he remembered—the eyes of the woman he had loved and lost. But there was no recognition in them. No spark of the bond they had shared for three all-too-short months six years ago.

Turning away, the woman helped a young girl into an austere horse-drawn buggy like those favored by the Amish in this part of Pennsylvania, and then she climbed up onto the seat beside the child. The adolescent driver flicked the reins, and the horses moved forward.

Frantically, Benjamin Miller tried to follow. The crowd of summer tourists on the main street of Peacock closed in around him. He jostled his way past one family, only to be boxed in by a busload of senior citizens in search of bargains on handmade quilts.

Dammit all! For almost six years, he'd been hoping he'd find Sarah again. Granted, he hadn't been searching the Amish countryside on a full-time basis. But he'd come looking anytime he'd been able to get away from the construction projects he supervised. As hard as Ben had tried, he'd been unable to get Sarah out of his mind.

Now that he'd finally found her, he wasn't going to let her go without finding out what had happened to her all those years ago. He desperately wanted to know why she had checked out of the hospital while he was unconscious without so much as leaving a message for him. How badly had she really been hurt in that motorcycle accident?

By the time he'd freed himself from the crowd on the sidewalk, the buggy was several blocks away and traveling at a fast clip. He'd never be able to catch them on foot.

He raced to the motorcycle that he'd parked in front of Seth Adams's feed store, a non-Amish merchant in town who was Ben's friend. Barely taking time to pull on his helmet, Ben twisted the ignition key in the Harley and backed the machine away from the curb—only to have a big tourist bus block his way.

"Aw, come on, man!" he shouted at the driver. "I need to get outta here."

But the bus was already disgorging its load of tourists, all of whom moved at the combined speed of a group of snails.

Gnashing his teeth in frustration, Ben wrestled his bike up onto the sidewalk, gunned it again, and snaked through clutches of screaming pedestrians until he could make his way back to the street. Then he roared after the buggy toward the highway.

He'd lost them.

To either side of the town, the highway stretched over the rolling countryside without a single buggy in sight.

His stomach knotted on the emptiness that had been there ever since he'd awakened without Sarah in his life.

Which way had the buggy turned? She couldn't have gotten far. He could almost smell her special herbal scent on the air, hear the soft murmur of her voice as she laughed at the antics of a child playing in the park, feel the softness of her lips on his. For six years, his dreams had been haunted by her. He wasn't going to lose her again. Not when this time he'd come so close.

Following his instincts, he turned right onto the highway and cruised slowly along the asphalt, checking the farms he passed, looking for a buggy. *One special buggy.*

THE PRICKLE OF UNEASE at Sarah Yoder's nape continued to taunt her most of the way home. It was as though the stranger were still watching her. A silly notion. No doubt his calling out her name was nothing more than a case of mistaken identity. There were dozens of Sarahs living in and around the small town of Peacock. And outsiders, bless their hearts, had a great deal of trouble telling one Amish woman from another.

Still, she'd turned to see if he was calling to her.

Though she hadn't gotten a good look at the man, their eyes had briefly met. An unexplainable image had popped into her mind bringing with it a sharp pain at her temple. How odd that she'd had a quick flash of flying down a highway at an unbelievable speed with the roar of a motorcycle in her ears. Even Amish boys who were testing their wings before they were baptized rarely purchased clandestine motorcycles—only dilapidated cars. And she'd certainly never ridden on a motorcycle that she could recall.

With a shake of her head, she glanced at her daughter and smiled.

"Ach, Becky, we will have to be doing the weeding when we get home," she said, speaking in the informal Pennsylvania Dutch dialect commonly used within the Amish community. "We'll want our garden filled with herbs when the healer comes."

Becky's quick grin revealed a row of evenly spaced baby teeth. "Will the healer teach me herbal remedies, too, Mama?"

Tucking some of the child's wayward strands of blond hair back under her organdy cap, Sarah said, "We'll see. But you are not to make a pest of yourself." Sarah's daughter was so bright, sometimes the child lacked the patience and humility necessary to fit comfortably into the community. Reining in Becky's enthusiasm seemed unnatural. But that was what Sarah must do if her daughter was to avoid being ostracized later on by her peers.

Once past a field of feed corn that stood shoulder

high, John Yoder, Sarah's youngest stepson, turned the buggy into the drive that fronted her three-story house. She had hoped to fill all those empty rooms with children of her own during her marriage to Amos but had only been blessed with Becky. And now that Amos had passed away, the boys had all moved out, leaving the house nearly silent. It was well Sarah would soon marry again. She needed to fill her hours with service to others in order to ignore a niggling sense that somewhere, somehow her life might have been different.

"You'll come in for a glass of something cold to drink?" she asked John.

"Nein, danke," he said, thanking her as he declined the offer. The boy had dark hair like his father and the faint trace of a beard was just beginning to show on his chin. "Eli wants my help with the haying."

"Visit when you can, then, and my thanks for the ride into town." Helping herself out of the buggy, and then assisting Becky, she went to the back of the open vehicle. She hefted two sacks of groceries from the back, mostly flour and other staples that she had picked up while delivering handmade quilts to the consignment store. "Say hello to your brothers for me?"

"I will." Clicking the reins, the boy turned the buggy in a tight circle and headed back up the lane.

"Safe home," Sarah called to him, wishing him a good trip, however short it might be.

As she walked up onto the porch, she heard the roar of a motorcycle in the distance. A slight shudder slid down her spine. Whyever was she suddenly giving so much thought to a machine entirely foreign to the way of life she had chosen?

For an instant—almost as if she were on that faraway motorcycle—she felt herself tipping dangerously. The back wheel skidded to the side. A telephone pole loomed in front of her. A scream rose in her throat, and she reached out to protect herself from certain collision.

In as a blink, the image was gone, replaced by the solid feel of her front porch beneath her feet.

Unsteady, Sarah grasped the porch railing.

"Mama? What's wrong?"

Looking down at her child, Sarah smiled. "I'm fine, Becky. Let's change into our work clothes. We've a lot to do." And Sarah's wayward imagination needed to be held in check.

BEN SPOTTED A BUGGY coming out of a farm lane and angled across the highway to meet it. The driver looked young enough to be the adolescent he'd seen with Sarah but he couldn't be sure. It was damn hard to tell the difference when all the Amish boys wore the same broadbrimmed straw hats and plain shirts with dark pants.

Slowing his Harley, Ben signaled the youngster to stop.

"Is this where Sarah Lapp lives?" he asked.

The boy stared at him so long, Ben began to think the kid was deaf, or had forgotten how to speak English. Perhaps the boy only spoke Pennsylvania Dutch?

"There is no Sarah Lapp here," the youngster finally said.

"Do you know of her?" Ben persisted, this time using the local language, which he'd picked up in his search for Sarah. He flicked up his helmet visor to get a better look at the boy. "I saw her in town—"

"If I knew of such a woman, I would not tell you. None of our women has a need for outsiders troubling them." The boy let go of the reins and reached toward something at his feet. "You are not welcome here."

"Now, wait a minute." Some punk kid, Amish or not, wasn't going to stop Ben from—

Ben's eyes widened as the boy produced a hunting rifle from under the buggy seat and rested it across his lap, pointing—almost casually—at Ben's gut.

"It is almost deer season," he said, looking past Ben toward a shady woods on the far side of the road. "Terrible thing, hunting accidents. One or two happen every year. A stranger would be wise to use care, particularly if he is in a place he should not be."

The kid just sat there, staring off into the distance. But Ben didn't have any trouble reading the threat. This youngster, in his misguided effort to protect the women in his community, might momentarily forget the Amish were supposed to be pacifists. And it would only take an instant.

Ben wasn't willing to risk his life when he wasn't

even sure this was Sarah's farm. For all Ben knew, this kid could be protecting his sister. Not Sarah.

And Sarah could have gotten on with her life without Ben, however much he might like to think otherwise.

What Ben needed was more information before he stuck out his neck.

"Okay, kid." Ben raised his hands in mock surrender. "I get the point." *For now.*

He wheeled his bike around and headed back toward town. If anybody could help him, Seth Adams could. Over the years, they'd become good friends, Seth providing insights into the community life the Amish lived from his perspective as an outsider. Meanwhile, Ben didn't mind losing a skirmish if eventually he could win the war.

HE PULLED UP IN FRONT of the feed store, killed the engine and sat there for a moment, trying to pull his thoughts together.

The kid had been lying. Ben was pretty sure of it. That was *his* Sarah he'd seen, and the boy had damn well known it. If that hadn't been the farm where Sarah lived, then he knew where she was.

"What's the trouble, Ben?" Dressed in overalls and a floppy hat, Seth wandered out of his store, grinning. "That ugly machine quit on you? Told you to get a horse."

"Nope. I've been chasing a dream."

Seth's eyebrows rose slightly. "That a fact?"

Briefly, Ben told Seth what he'd been up to and how he was more convinced than ever that Sarah

Lapp was somewhere nearby. "Are you absolutely sure you don't know her?"

"Like I told you before, half the folks around here are named Lapp and the other half are Yoders. And most every woman has a biblical name like Sarah or Mary or some such. You telling me her name's Sarah doesn't help overly much."

Ben struggled to remember some other way *his* Sarah could be identified—the Sarah he'd spotted in the buggy. "She's got a little girl with her, maybe four or five years old. And there was a kid driving the buggy, maybe sixteen or so, who just happened to have a hunting rifle with him." Describing their clothing wouldn't do any good. All the Amish dressed identically, or nearly so. The personal things he knew about Sarah wouldn't help Seth to identify her, either—the delicate shape of her ears, the taste of her full lips, the fine pattern of veins on her breasts marred only by a tiny strawberry mark above her left nipple.

"Let me think," Seth said, scratching at his two days worth of whiskers as he gazed off in the direction of the highway that ran past the town. "Don't know for sure but that could be 'Forgetful Sarah' you're talking about."

"*Forgetful* Sarah?"

"Yep. Since their names are so much alike, most everybody in these parts has a nickname, sorta like a secret code they use among themselves. There's Thick Joseph and Beanbag. Some of 'em use their pa's name, like Eli's John. If that woman is who I think she is, they call her 'Forgetful Sarah.'"

"That sounds damn odd to me."

"Not really. Seems a few years back, she went away for a while and forgot she'd promised to marry Amos Yoder."

Something painful slammed into Ben's gut. "You mean she's married?" *His* Sarah? He should have known but the news still hurt.

"*Was.* Her old man passed on a year or so ago. Prettiest widow around, I'd guess. That's her little girl you seen. Cute as a button, she is. And smart, too. The boy driving was likely one of her stepsons."

Dear God, during all the years he'd been dreaming about Sarah, she'd been married and having another man's baby, raising another man's children.

Ben chided himself for being surprised. *You didn't really think she'd wait for you all this time, did you, chump?*

But he'd waited for her. Not for a minute had he been able to get her out of his mind. Not while he'd worked his way up to foreman and superintendent, and finally buying into a partnership in one of the biggest construction companies on the East Coast. He'd always remembered *his* Sarah.

Now that he knew she'd gone on with her life, he'd be smart to ride his Harley back to Philadelphia, avoiding macho kids with rifles. Philly was where he belonged.

"I heard she never did remember what she'd been doing while she was gone. Fact is, I imagine her folks were just plain happy to have her back home again safe and sound."

Ben stared at Seth incredulously. "Are you saying Sarah had amnesia?"

"Still does, I guess. Not that anybody cares after all this time."

Ben lifted his helmet off and speared his fingers through his hair, so long it hung past his shoulders. It was hot and humid with only a light breeze disturbing the heavy August air. The bike accident that had put Ben in the hospital had injured Sarah, too. The nurses hadn't told him she had lost her memory. Maybe they didn't even know. They'd only said that her parents had come for her.

"Heard tell," Seth continued when Ben didn't speak, "that she's fixin' to marry again real soon. Another widower, this one with a passel of kids for her to raise up like she did Amos's boys. Must be she likes being a mom."

She was about to marry for a second time? If Ben let that happen, she'd be lost to him forever. Maybe, just maybe, he'd been given one last chance. *If* he could convince her the love they'd once felt for each other—the love she'd forgotten— was still there.

"Seth, I need to see her. To talk to her. I can't let her marry some other guy without at least—"

"Now don't go getting yourself all in a dander, son. You can't go roaring into some old Amish farm and make off with one of their womenfolk. They might be peaceable, but they won't stand for that."

"Tell me about it," Ben muttered, thinking of Sarah's stepson and his hunting rifle. "But what can I do? I need a chance to talk to her, get to know her and help her remember the past. If I let her marry some other man, there isn't a chance in Hades we'll ever get back together again. I love her, Seth. You know these people. What can I do?''

"That's a hard thing to say, son.''

"I'm tempted to just ride right up that farmhouse and kidnap her. That's what I'd like to do.'' In a way, Sarah's family had kidnapped her from Ben. Reversing the tables on them seemed only fair.

"Likely that would get you put in jail,'' Seth said. "Particularly since Forgetful Sarah doesn't know you from Adam.''

Ben wanted to argue with Seth's logic but he couldn't. "Maybe I could go to the head of her church, get him to see reason about me and Sarah getting back together again.''

Barking a laugh, Seth shook his head. "That's not likely to work worth beans, what with her planning to marry a member of the congregation real soon.''

Real soon! Dammit! Ben had to come up with a plan and do it in a hurry. "There's got to be something I can do,'' he said, his jaw aching as he gritted his teeth.

Seth studied the tip of his work boot, then stared off across the street. "Forgetful Sarah's been wanting to learn folk healing but there's nobody 'round here that can teach her.''

"Yeah, that sounds like my Sarah. She was studying to be a nurse when we had that accident I told you about.'' She'd been so committed to learning to help others, Sarah had sacrificed all contact with her Amish roots. She'd rebelled against many of their beliefs, too, including the stricture against falling in love with an outsider.

"The bishop of the local congregation asked if I'd drive on up to Plymouth when it was time and bring the healer back to stay a spell with Sarah."

"I thought the Amish didn't believe in cars."

"They're not allowed to own or drive 'em once they've been baptized, but if they need to, riding along doesn't bother 'em none."

Hoping he'd someday have a chance to put his knowledge to use, Ben had made it a point to learn both the customs and the language of the Amish people. But sometimes he got confused, the logic of their rules escaping him. Just as they hadn't always made sense to Sarah.

"I love my parents," she had once said, fighting a periodic case of homesickness. "But just because I want to be a nurse, I'll never see them again. It's not fair."

With the back of his hand, Ben brushed a few strands of hair from her face. "You could go back home and rejoin the church." He held his breath waiting for her answer.

She looked at him, tears pooling in her eyes. "No, Benjamin, this is where I belong—with you. It's just that sometimes I miss my home."

Sighing in relief, he touched her lips with a quick kiss. "I know you do. But we'll make our own home someday. A big ole house with lots of room for your garden and a dozen rooms for our children. I promise.''

Ben was still trying to keep that promise and as close as he'd suddenly come to her, it didn't look as if that was going to be easy. ''So about this healer,'' he said to Seth. ''What does that have to do with me getting to Sarah?''

''Could be, if I brought this healer to stay with Sarah now instead of later—'' he winked at Ben ''—you could get reacquainted 'fore she ties the knot again.''

''You want me to *pretend* to be a faith healer?''

''It might work. And damned if I can think of any other way to get you on the inside without rousing all the Amish menfolk about you being there.''

''Okay,'' Ben said cautiously, not in the least eager to be shot by Sarah's overly conscientious stepson. ''If I wore their kind of clothes and got myself a fake beard, maybe I could carry it off for a few days. I don't know much about herbs but I've had a lot of advanced first aid training. At least I could fake it long enough for me and Sarah to get acquainted again.''

''Yep. Might work that way. Problem is, though, a man healer usually teaches a new female, and vice versa, this time it's a woman coming to help out Sarah. Seems like there's a real shortage of healers these days and the preachers gave 'em a special dispensation for one woman to teach another. Fannie Raber's the healer's name.''

'' 'Fannie'?'' Ben stared at the older man incredulously. ''Are you suggesting I'm going to have to masquerade as a *woman*?'' He almost shouted the word. He was six feet tall and all man. No one would believe he was a woman!

Seth shrugged. ''Them outfits the women wear aren't exactly sexy. They cover up real good. With a set of falsies—''

''Jeez! And just what do you suggest I do about all these whiskers that keep popping out?'' he asked, rubbing his hand over his face.

''You're pretty fair complected and haven't got much of a beard. Shaving a couple or three times a day oughta do it.''

The man was insane. He had to be. The thought of Ben Miller dressed up in a skirt and bonnet was ludicrous. No way could he pass for a woman even with a set of falsies. And he sure as hell didn't want to try. If the news ever got back to the guys who worked for him, they'd razz him for the rest of his life.

On the other hand, could he actually go on living knowing he hadn't tried everything within his power to get Sarah back? He'd been raised by a father who thought breakfast ought to be a pint of gin and a mother who thought being called slovenly was a compliment. In Sarah, Ben had found goodness and a gentle spirit he hadn't known existed. She'd been the one who had motivated him to get his contractor's license. She'd *believed* in him when he hadn't even believed in himself.

The answer to his question was easier than he had expected. And more appalling.

Ah, hell! He could only hope nobody in Philadelphia, including the bankers who regularly loaned his company millions of dollars for construction projects, ever heard about the stunt he was about to pull.

THE STOREKEEPER HANDED Ben a white organdy cap like those the Amish women wore. He stared at it dubiously. Most days he wore a hard hat, or carried a briefcase if he had a meeting in town. Putting this little dinky thing on his head was going to feel weird. Though no stranger than being strapped into a size 40-D bra stuffed with foam rubber. But then, wearing the sacklike dress Seth's wife had custom made for him was odd, too. Particularly since he had to use straight pins to hold the bib apron in place. This sect of Amish people had something against modern inventions like buttons, at least so far as women's dresses were concerned.

"You really think I can get away with this masquerade?" Ben asked, studying his image in the full-length mirror. The long sleeves mostly covered his hairy arms and the bib apron disguised the shape of his physique—which frankly looked a little lopsided with the falsies on.

"You were the one who said you'd try anything to get close to Forgetful Sarah."

He had, and he'd meant it. But in the two days it had taken to make this dress, he'd had major second thoughts. The grandma-grump black oxford shoes mashing his toes together didn't help the situation, either. Thank God Amish women didn't wear three-inch heels.

Putting the cap on, he tucked his shoulder-length hair that he'd pulled back in a ponytail up under the bonnet and pulled the hat forward enough to cover his sideburns, tying the drawstrings under his chin. If he managed to get away with this masquerade, he damn well ought to go into showbiz.

"Well, aren't you the sweetest little lady, Fannie Raber?" Seth crowed, nearly splitting his gut with laughter.

"Knock it off, Seth, or you'll be eating this bonnet."

The storekeeper's chuckles sputtered to a halt. "All I can say is I hope this little lady of yours has a good sense of humor. She's gonna need it."

Grimacing, Ben saw little that was humorous about his situation. But he did recall Sarah's quiet laughter when something struck her as funny and the bright shine in her blue eyes when she was happy. Little things had meant so much to her—a rose still blooming when the first snow fell, an electric train circling a miniature village in a store window at Christmas, wind blowing in her face as she rode behind him on his bike. He wanted her to experience all of that again—with him.

Normally, he was a pretty straightforward guy. He spoke his mind. He didn't keep secrets. But the thought of that hunting rifle pointed at his middle gave Ben second thoughts.

So did the possibility that Sarah might not want him back in her life.

Dammit. More than anything else, he wanted a second chance. If the price was masquerading as a woman, so be it. It'd be easier living with that than knowing he hadn't given it his best shot.

"Well, we'd better be on our way, son. No sense keeping the lady waiting."

Automatically, Ben checked his watch—and discovered his wrist was empty. An Amish woman wouldn't wear a watch at all, much less one with a wide gold band and a mechanism that supplied enough information on its face to synchronize a military assault. To cover his slip, he tugged the sleeve of his dress down to his wrist.

A bad case of nerves, like the first time he'd gone up fifty floors in an open elevator, twisted through Ben's gut. Seth had sent word to Sarah that he'd be delivering Fannie Raber to her doorstep that afternoon. The healer from up north would be staying awhile. Everything should be ready.

As they walked out of the store, Seth eyed Ben sideways. "You still got your pants on, son?"

"Damn right, I do," he muttered. "I used your scissors to turn my spare pair jeans into cutoffs. No way am I gonna have some breeze catch this fool skirt and show my privates."

Seth's booming laughter rocketed up and down Peacock's main street, making the tourists turn their heads. Stepping off the porch, Ben twisted his ankle in the low-heel oxford shoes and nearly fell flat on his face before he caught himself.

Masquerading as a woman was going to be a hell of a lot harder than he'd expected. But he simply hadn't come up with another alternative to get close to Sarah.

Off and on over the past six years, Ben had traveled most of the rural back roads of Amish country in both Pennsylvania and Ohio looking for her. The neat farms with their whitewashed buildings and orderly rows of crops were familiar to him. He gave the people plenty of credit for hard work.

But they'd also kept Sarah away from him.

Time and again he'd stopped a farmer plowing a field to ask if he knew Sarah Lapp. Or he'd questioned a woman walking to a neighbor's house. Never once had they so much as hinted she lived nearby. In their clannish ways, they'd kept *his* Sarah a secret—just as Sarah's stepson had denied her existence only days ago.

And now Ben was scared that secrecy had been *her* idea.

Seth pulled his stake truck off the main road into a lane leading to a house that looked very much like every other one they had passed—the farm where the boy had threatened Ben two days ago.

The fields were well tended, the barn well kept. Nearby a tall silo waited for this year's harvest. It wasn't exactly the community where Sarah grew up but it was damn close, maybe thirty miles away. A long buggy ride, he supposed, but practically neighbors from his perspective.

As they stopped in front of the house, a woman stepped out onto the porch. A welcoming smile played at the corners of her lips, not dimmed in the least by the austere navy blue dress she wore or the little cap covering her flaxen hair.

All of the powerful memories that had driven Ben for the past six years washed over him. The way she had welcomed him home each night—and greeted him, sleepy-eyed in the morning. The caress of her lips on his. Her incredible honesty, in his arms and in her life. Her ability to make him feel like a king with only a fleeting glance and a smile.

In that one breathtaking instant, he knew he'd done the right thing by coming here—even in this outlandish costume.

In time, Sarah would remember him.

And, he hoped, would love him again.

Chapter Two

In response to a sudden throbbing in her head, Sarah rubbed the faint scar at her temple with her fingertips.

What an extraordinarily large woman, she thought, as the healer stepped out of Seth's truck. Such broad shoulders. And there was little in her features that could be described as soft or feminine. Sarah had certainly expected someone older. This woman was...*robust,* to say the least.

But Fannie Raber was a well-respected healer, Sarah reminded herself. Someone valued by the community. In her heart Sarah aspired to that same humble position.

Becky pushed open the screen door behind Sarah and latched onto her leg. "Mama, is that the healer?"

"Yes, she's the one." She hooked her arm protectively over her daughter's shoulder. In tandem, they walked down the porch steps. "You're welcome, Fannie Raber," she said, her gaze perusing a face that seemed oddly familiar, yet why that should be, Sarah wasn't sure. "Please think of our home as yours."

"Sarah, it's good to see you." The stranger spoke in a husky voice that resonated like a familiar chord within Sarah. Perhaps it was Fannie's distinctively rich tone that contained the power to heal along with her knowledge of herbs, she mused.

"And I you, Fannie." For an instant, another name formed on Sarah's lips but went unspoken. In the healer's sky-blue eyes, she saw the offer of friendship…and a puzzling sense of something deeper. Something mesmerizing. Something Sarah wasn't sure she dared to pursue. "I hope your journey here was a comfortable one," she said, trying to ease her strange reaction.

"The trail I followed was far longer and more twisted than I had hoped," the healer said with an ambiguous lift of her pale brows.

"Yes, well… You're here now."

"At long last."

Seth shoved the small black suitcase into Ben's chest, rousing him from his intense scrutiny of Sarah. She hadn't changed much in six years. Her heart-shaped face and gently arched brows were as familiar to him as the image he saw every morning in the mirror—or the one he dreamed about every night. Her lips, naturally curving into a smile, were as known to him as his own. Even after all this time, she'd aged little, her cheeks still as smooth and bright as a fresh peach.

His hands clenched against the need to touch her—just once.

"Looks like you folks will be gettin' along fine," Seth said. "I'll be on my way then."

Sarah's gaze flicked to the storekeeper. "*Danke,* Seth, for bringing Fannie."

"My pleasure, ma'am." With a grin, he tipped his hat to her, then returned to the driver's side of the truck. A moment later he drove away.

It was all Ben could do not to burst out with the truth about who he really was. But if Sarah didn't remember him—and obviously she didn't—forcing the issue would probably scare her to death. He'd have to go slow, demonstrate a lot more patience than was his usual style.

He hunkered down to eye level in front of the little girl. "What's your name, honey?" Though he tried to talk like a soprano, his voice came out sounding like a tenor with a sore throat.

Her gaze met his steadily, her eyes a shade or two lighter than her mother's, the hair peeking out from under her organdy cap slightly darker.

"Rebecca Yoder, but Mama calls me Becky."

"May I call you Becky, too?"

"Are you going to teach me to grind up herbs and such to make people all better?"

"I'll certainly give it a try." And he hoped what he knew about first aid would help him get by. He didn't know much about being a woman, either, except this damn dress was hotter than Hades and the bra straps kept slipping off his shoulders.

"Becky," Sarah scolded gently. "Let's give Fannie a chance to settle in before we badger her about the lessons."

The child continued to stare at Ben. "Aunt Edna has a nose even bigger than yours and she's got a wart right on the end of it. 'Cept we aren't supposed to say nothin' about it. Mama says mentioning people's *de*-fects isn't polite."

"Becky!"

Choking back a laugh, Ben stood.

"I'm so sorry." Looking chagrined, Sarah apologized. "Sometimes my daughter is a little too honest. She's old enough that she should know better."

Properly chastised, Becky hung her head and peeked up at him through lowered lashes. She was a cute little minx with the same devilish glimmer he'd often seen in her mother's eyes—like the time when he'd had to unwrap ten boxes, one inside the other, before he got to the new pair of work gloves she'd given him for Christmas.

"Don't worry about it," Ben assured them both, remembering that had been the best Christmas he'd ever had.

A frown pleating her smooth forehead, Sarah gestured toward the front door. "Please, come in. Make yourself at home. I've made some lemonade for you."

"Great." A tall glass of beer would have been better, but Ben figured he'd have to do without that for the duration of his stay.

Ben stepped into the house, pleasantly surprised by what he found. He appreciated good workmanship. This old house had been crafted by the best. The plank flooring fit together with hardly a groove showing, the doorways were perfectly plumb and the furniture in the large living room was simple but sturdy. A hint of lemon scented the air as though Sarah had been cleaning. Her personal fragrance was an herbal one, like the chamomile tea she used to drink in the evening as she studied her books or cuddled close to him.

"Nice house," he commented, wishing they could go back in time. He'd held on to their old apartment, subletting it, his name still on the mailbox, just in case she'd come looking for him. Now he lived in a stately five-bedroom Victorian he'd been restoring on an acre of land. But without Sarah, without a family, it was too empty, the project slow-going.

She preceded him up the stairs to the second floor and Becky tagged along behind. "The house has been in my husband's family for years. I've tried to keep it nice since he's been gone."

"Do you still miss him?" Ben could have bitten his tongue for having asked such a stupid question. Of course, she did. She'd married the man, hadn't she?

She paused at the top landing, turning toward him, her expression thoughtful. "Amos was a good man. The house is quiet now with him gone and the boys moved out and only Becky and me left."

"So you only miss the noise he made?" Ben teased, his heart threatening to break. No one had ever missed him. Not even Sarah.

For a moment, she looked startled by his question and then smiled, shrugging. "Perhaps."

Ben could have jumped for joy. No way had

Sarah loved her husband. She was capable of great passion. If she'd been grieving for Amos, Ben would have seen it in her eyes. Then he remembered she was about to marry some other guy. How could she so easily forget what they'd had together and play musical chairs with other men as though they meant nothing to her?

"This will be your room," she said, stopping in front of an open doorway.

He glanced inside. Except for a handmade quilt that covered a narrow bed, the room was as plain as the rest of the house. "Where do you sleep?"

"Across the hall. If you need anything, you have only to call."

His gaze slid in that direction, to a larger, more inviting bed. Sunlight spilled across the diamond-pattern quilt. He doubted Sarah would be willing to give him what he needed just yet—even if she did remember him. But she would, eventually, if he had any luck at all.

"My room's down there." Becky pointed toward the end of the hallway. "My brothers used to live here, too, but they moved to Adam's house when he married Beiler's Sue. She's real pretty. He used to sneak out at night to see her but we're not s'posed to talk about that, either."

Ben lifted his eyebrows.

Sarah cupped her recalcitrant daughter's shoulder, applying a warning bit of pressure. "Please take your time putting your things away and washing up. Whenever you're ready, I have lemonade for you."

With a parting smile, Sarah marched Becky downstairs. She didn't need to tell the child that she'd spoken out of turn. Her daughter frequently did just that and however many admonishments she'd been given, nothing seemed to sway her. "Out of the mouths of babes," they said. In an Amish settlement, silence was often more valued than words.

Sending Becky outside with still another warning to behave herself, Sarah checked the pitcher of lemonade in the gasoline-driven refrigerator and sighed.

She'd felt curiously uncomfortable standing in the hallway with Fannie. Perhaps it was her size that was somewhat daunting. Or the strong angles of her features. If Sarah hadn't known better, she would have thought the woman was a man. But, of course, no Amish bishop would have sent a man to stay with her—not when Sarah was an unattached widow. And Seth wouldn't have delivered such a person. So certainly Fannie was a woman and a well-known healer in her northern community, whatever else Sarah's instincts might be telling her.

And what Fannie no doubt needed, given her mannish features, was Sarah's sympathy. Not her suspicions. Like Sarah's dear friend Short Martha, no woman should be judged on her stature alone.

Over the years, Sarah had made herself bend to the will of the community. On more days than she'd care to remember, obedience had been difficult. During her youth she'd wanted to rebel, to resist the pressure of the community to conform. A foolish, short-sighted notion that could only have brought grief. And terrible, dark shame.

Shivering, she refused to even think about what might have happened if she'd followed a rebellious path.

She was grateful for her parents' firm hand and Amos's wisdom that had kept her on course. The fact that she occasionally still chafed under the constraints of her daily life only reflected on her own weakness and rebellious nature.

She bent her head, much like Becky had when she'd been chastised upstairs. Like a lightning strike, an image flashed through her mind. It vanished so quickly she barely had a chance to register the likeness of the man before it was gone. Almost forgotten.

She blinked and rubbed her temple. Whatever was the matter with her? The illusive impression she'd seen was of no man she had ever known. She didn't even want to know such a man. He was too male, too forceful. Soon she would marry Samuel Mast. The community expected that of her. She expected it of herself. She'd already bent her will to the community once. She would do so again.

Her head snapped up at the sound of a bellowed curse from upstairs.

My sakes! Whatever could be the matter with Fannie to shout such a blasphemy? Sarah raced for the stairs, grateful her daughter was well out of hearing. Her small ears picked up too much as it was—which she was all too quick to repeat.

Fannie was in the hallway, muttering, and snatching at the waist of her bib apron.

"What's the matter?" Sarah asked.

"One of these da-darn pins stuck me. I can't seem to find—"

"Here, let me."

"No, it's all right. I can do it."

But Sarah knew how frustrating it was to get a straight pin tangled in the folds of her skirt and not be able to find the troublesome source of being pricked, so she proceeded to pluck away at Fannie's skirt.

When Sarah touched the woman, Fannie drew a quick breath. "You don't have to—"

Discovering the offending pin, Sarah reset it safely in the cloth, and it was a good thing. For a minute, the poor woman had sounded ready to choke.

Sarah lifted her gaze. "There you are...." Her words trailed off as a pair of pale blue eyes snared her with such intensity she nearly gasped. Unfamiliar heat flooded her body, embarrassing her as her nipples puckered and her heart rate accelerated to a distressing pace. Fearful Fannie might misunderstand her reaction, Sarah stepped back.

Fannie's lips hitched into the faintest suggestion of a smile. "I've always hoped the church would decide to let us use safety pins, but no such luck."

Still stunned by her response to Fannie, Sarah suppressed a responding smile at the rebellious thought the healer had expressed—one she'd often considered herself.

"Yes, well..." Flustered, her heart beating erratically, she turned away. "It is the wisdom of the bishop we try to follow."

AFTER THEY HAD FINISHED their lemonades, Ben followed Sarah outside. It was just as well she seemed anxious to show him her garden. Inside the house, her closeness had felt too intimate, too tempting. And when she'd touched him to fix that stupid pin—even if it had been through several layers of cotton—Ben had very nearly lost it. He'd wanted so much to touch her, hold her—he'd ached with it. Damn, it had been so long since he'd held her in his arms!

And he'd damn well better watch his language, too.

He'd nearly forgotten how much she objected to his cursing—words that came as second nature around a construction site and just as often in business meetings. When they'd lived together, he'd managed to clean up his vocabulary. He guessed he'd have to do it again.

"Do you have any herbs you find especially helpful?" she asked, interrupting his thoughts.

He glanced down the neat rows of what looked like weeds. "Guess that depends on what's wrong with the patient," he hedged.

"Yes, of course." She knelt, fingering some big old dandelions, her movements so graceful she could have been a dancer. "For a time, dandelion root seemed to help Amos's high blood pressure. But I guess it wasn't enough."

"Some things we just can't cure."

"I've found echinacea to be helpful for sore throats. Thyme, too, of course."

"Sounds to me you already know a lot about the healing arts."

"Only what is common knowledge in the community. I had hoped—" Rising, she looked at him with achingly beautiful eyes, as blue as a mountain lake on a sunny day. "I thought you might have some specialized knowledge of women's troubles."

He swallowed hard. "'Wo-men's troubles'?" His voice cracked.

"After Becky was born, I wasn't able to conceive again. I tried damiana leaf but it didn't seem to help. I'm soon to be married—"

"'Damiana'?" he echoed, his falsetto voice dropping a half octave in surprise. He'd heard about that stuff on a late-night talk show. It was supposed to, well, get a woman all hot and bothered for her man. He didn't know if it worked or not but Sarah sure hadn't needed any of that with him!

Nodding, she pursed her lips and her chin trembled slightly. "I was hoping—"

"You want to have more babies?"

"Very much, yes."

He hitched up his shoulder, trying to get his slipping bra strap back in place. By damn, he'd be willing to fill her belly with all the babies she wanted. But, of course, it wasn't his place. Some other man would have that pleasure unless Ben could convince Sarah that the love they'd shared had endured in spite of her amnesia. And how the hell could he do that when he was clopping around in awkward black shoes and dressed like a woman?

"Naturally, my primary goal is to help others," she hastily added. "But if it is possible that I be blessed again with a child…"

Unable to resist, he touched her cheek with his fingertips. So soft. So sweet. "You'll have your babies. I'll see to it." He'd move heaven and earth to give Sarah whatever she wanted. He could only hope he'd be the one to father her children.

Her eyes glistened with unshed tears. "Thank you, Fannie. That you believe it is possible I may conceive again gives me the faith I need."

Instinctively, he leaned forward. Toward her lips. Into the fresh herbal scent of her.

Into deep trouble.

The moment her eyes widened, he backed off.

Well, hell! She must think he was a real wacko. He'd likely never get the knack of playing a woman right. Not that he had any desire to make this masquerade a long-term proposition.

He was definitely going to have to take this charade one step at a time. But it wasn't going to be easy, particularly when merories of their time together came to him unbidden, memories like their first kiss.

She'd been staying in his apartment for nearly six weeks. "Just friends" he'd told her, and he'd been a damned saint for the whole time, not once touching her. And then one morning she'd been making biscuits for breakfast, and flour had streaked the softness of her cheek. He'd brushed it away, just as he'd touched her today. And then he'd kissed her.

Her lips had melted like soft butter, molding to his. Opening for him. She'd tasted like the sweetness of heaven and the bliss of coming home. Her tongue had shyly teased with his.

He'd been scared and excited and aroused by her innocence, afraid he'd frighten her if he went too fast. So he'd just kissed her, not pressing her for more, and when she'd moaned low in her throat, he'd backed off.

Her eyes were wide, a darker blue than usual, and he thought she might want him almost as much as he wanted her.

"You okay?" he whispered.

"Oh, yes, Benjamin. I'm quite well." She smiled and a glint of mischief appeared in her eyes. "If I had known kissing was so pleasant, I might not have waited so long to try it."

A rush of masculine pride filled Ben's chest. "That was your first kiss?"

She nodded.

"The guys where you come from must be crazy—or blind. I've wanted to do that since the first night we met."

"And you are the first man I have wished would kiss me. It has taken you so long, I wondered if you did not find me attractive."

He sputtered a laugh, gathering her into his arms at last. She fit as if she'd been made especially for him. "You're the sexiest woman I've ever known, Sweet Sarah. And I've been driving myself crazy trying *not* to kiss you. Now that I know you like it, I think I'm never gonna stop.'' He kissed her again, and that morning was the first time he'd ever been late for work. For all he'd cared, his boss, Mac Culdane, could have docked him a week's worth of pay and it still would have been worth every penny. All he could think about was coming home that night—coming home to his Sarah.

A QUILTIING BEE

The night of Ben's arrival, Sarah's huge living room was crammed full of women hovering over quilts stretched on wooden frames. As they stitched, they buzzed about the latest recipe they'd tried and the man in a neighboring community who'd been injured in a threshing accident. As the evening had grown late, Becky had been sent upstairs to bed.

The evening had already gone on for far too long for Ben's taste, too. These women kept quizzing him on ''women's'' troubles. *Consulting* with him as a healer. Looking for answers he certainly didn't have. If only they'd asked him about plumbing codes or the going interest rate for construction loans, he could have handled that. But not *women's* troubles.

''My Madeline started her monthlies some time back,'' an angular woman confided. ''*Ach,* she has a terrible time with them, she does.''

Ben's face flushed hot, and he pricked his finger with the needle he'd been toying with. He made an effort to contribute to the conversation. ''That's too bad.''

"Tried most everything I could think to do, but so far nothing seems to help."

Sucking the blood from his finger, he nodded noncommittally. Apparently Sarah had invited the ladies over to meet and greet him—her—on his first evening in the community. He really wished she hadn't done that.

"Course, I had a hard time before I had babies, too. Could be female troubles run in the family, *ja?*" Without looking up, the woman next to him made a dozen neat little stitches along the edge of a pink diamond.

He didn't want to know this. He really didn't. And he couldn't imagine how anyone could see what they were doing in the flare of the kerosene lamps hung around the room. Hadn't these people ever heard of electricity? How sinful could it be, he wondered, if a decent light prevented blindness? But, of course, he couldn't complain. Not out loud. He was supposed to be as Amish as all these ladies were.

From across the quilting frame, a woman said, "I just send my girls to bed with a hot-water bottle. Seems to work fine for them."

Ben wanted to crawl *under* a bed.

He glanced across the room to where Sarah was diligently working on another quilt. She smiled—a soft, gentle smile meant just for him—and he wanted to whisk her off to bed. The two of them together. Upstairs. Alone.

"Tell us, Fannie," a plump woman of forty asked, "what news of Plymouth?"

"'Plymouth'?" he echoed.

"*Ja*, how are the Stoltzfus family getting on?"

"Oh, ah, fine," he said, belatedly remembering the visiting healer was supposed to be from that northern community.

"And Una's Tess? She's well?"

"Ah, yes, she's well." Or maybe she died. How was he supposed to know?

"*Ach*, it is amazing after all that woman went through." The plump woman ducked her head to her work again. "The doctors taking her insides out and all after the faith healing failed. Thought she might not survive."

"Yes, well..." Darting his gaze around the room in the futile hope of escape, he cleared his throat. "Modern medicine has its place."

The conversation flowed all around him, and Ben tried desperately to appear inconspicuous. They talked about husbands and children, planting crops and favorite recipes. Ben couldn't contribute much to the conversation.

Restless he started to plow his fingers through his hair but the fool organdy cap he had to wear was in his way. How the devil did a woman scratch her scalp if she got an itch?

An older woman across the way giggled in response to her friend's comment about attentive husbands. "I remember when I was first married, we had such a cold snap, my husband's 'thingie' had shrunk up so bad, I thought he'd lost it."

The women thought that was hilarious.

Ben thought it was scary.

"Later that night he tried to tell me everything was all right," the woman went on, starting a new round of giggles. "But it didn't look any different to me!"

The women practically fell off their chairs, they were laughing so hard.

Ben didn't laugh. Instead he began to sweat. He couldn't do this. Men weren't supposed to find themselves in the middle of a female gabfest. Any minute now, someone would notice he didn't belong. The only reason someone—including Sarah—hadn't already blown the whistle on him was that they *expected* him to be the visiting healer. So that's what they saw. Human nature, he supposed, was on his side this time.

"Looks to me like you got all the extra doses of growing juice that were meant for me."

Turning, Ben found a woman about four feet tall standing next to him. Her head was too big for her body, and her arms too short. Though she was a dwarf—not an uncommon occurrence in some Amish communities—her grin was about as big and friendly as any he'd ever seen.

"Doesn't seem quite fair, does it?" he commented. Distractedly, he hitched up his slipping bra strap.

"No sense in arguing with what life gives you." She eyed him with a decided twinkle.

He nodded. "Yes, ma'am."

"Other days, a body would have to say Mother Nature's got quite a sense of humor." She rested her hand next to his on the quilt, her fingers short and stubby compared to his. "Name's Martha— Short Martha to those who know me."

"Pleased to meet you, Short Martha."

"Maybe. Maybe not. Not much gets by me, Fannie Raber. Being so short, folks have a way of ignoring me."

"I wouldn't think of ignoring you." He wouldn't dare. The woman had already seen through him. He was sure of it. Dammit, he knew he wouldn't be able to pull off this masquerade.

"On the other hand, Forgetful Sarah's been a good friend to me. I care about her."

"So do I, Martha," he said softly with all the sincerity he could muster.

"I wouldn't want to see her hurt."

Shaking his head, he said, "Neither would I."

"She's a lucky woman to be marrying Samuel Mast in a month's time, she is. No finer farmer she'll be finding, or a better man, either."

Ben swallowed hard. "I'm glad to hear that."

"Are you?" Martha studied him a moment more, her gaze amazingly intense, and then she shrugged. "Surely do hope you're better at healing than you are at quilting." With a happy, cackling laugh, she wandered back to her place at the adjacent quilt.

Ben felt as if he'd just escaped a bullet. Or maybe he'd made an ally. At this point, he couldn't tell. But he sure hoped this quilting bee would end soon.

HAVING FELT EDGY ALL evening, Sarah was grateful when the ladies departed, their menfolk picking them up in their buggies after returning from a visit to Samuel's house down the road. She'd have to say Fannie hadn't contributed much to the quilting effort, but the healer had been accepted by all of Sarah's friends.

That should have given her a sense of relief. Curiously, it didn't seem to ease her disquieting feelings.

She sat heavily in the simple pine rocking chair Amos had made for her and rubbed at her temples. Why on earth was she so troubled by Fannie's presence?

"You look like you could use a massage."

Sarah started to get up but Fannie's hands closed over her shoulders, pressing her down again. She felt the healer kneading the tight muscles of her neck and shoulders.

"I'm all right," she protested.

"I'm a healer, remember? I know when someone has more stress than they can handle."

She wanted to argue, but Fannie's hands were very talented. Taut muscles eased under their insistent pressure, and Sarah felt herself relaxing in a way she hadn't experienced before. She breathed deeply.

"Do you remember the accident you had?" Fannie asked, her voice as soothing as her hands. "The one when you hurt your head?"

"Hmm." Her eyelids felt incredibly heavy. "I remember waking up in a hospital."

"Just before the accident, do you remember what you were doing?"

"Not really." Beneath her fluttering eyelids, scenery blinked by in a blur. Imaginary. As illusive as a cloud.

"How 'bout where you were living?"

An image of a tall building flashed into her mind. A brick building. Totally unfamiliar.

She frowned. "I lived with my family until I married Amos."

"Are you sure?"

The voice from behind her was low and slightly rough, hauntingly familiar. And persuasive. She wanted to confess whatever sins of omission or commission Fannie desired of her. And she'd do it, too, as soon as she had the energy.

But instead she felt herself drifting, lost in a dream that she'd never quite forgotten.

A dream that came back to her now.

Chapter Three

The pack of hoodlums had cornered her like wild beasts circling their prey.

"Hey, Amish, where ya goin'?" the leader taunted.

Fearfully, Sarah glanced from one man to the next, each with a bandanna roping his head and tattoos marking his arms. Streetlights cast dark shadows on their faces and into the doorways of shops closed for the night. Lost, she was. No more than a block or two from the bus terminal, and she'd taken a wrong turn. She'd been warned not to come to the city. But she'd wanted to so much...

"Please, I've done you no harm." Panic threatened and she trembled. "Let me pass."

She stepped forward and another man crowded her, snatching her cap from her head. She grabbed for it but he twirled it around on his fingertip just out of her reach.

"How 'bout you and me go have some fun?" he chided, smirking.

"Yeah, we'll show you a good time," another one added.

Someone made a grab for her suitcase—containing all of her worldly possessions—and she pulled it back. Fear pounded through her veins. Her throat constricted on a silent scream and her mouth went as dry as toast. They'd been right, her family and friends. She never should have left home. Rebellion, becoming worldly—even pursuing an education—would lead only to darkness and shame.

Suddenly a roaring noise penetrated her senses, the revving of an engine, and a motorcycle bounced up over the curb onto the sidewalk. The driver angled the machine between her and the gang of cutthroats.

"These fellows bothering you, lady?" he asked. He didn't look in her direction but focused on the hooligans instead. Long, blond hair streamed down his back from beneath his helmet. A black leather jacket stretched across broad shoulders and faded jeans molded over powerful thighs.

"I just want them to let me go," she said, her throat aching with fear.

"They'll be happy to do that, won't you, gentlemen?"

"Bug off, creep," the man with her cap said.

"You're trespassing," the gang leader warned.

The biker revved his engine again. "I'm askin' you real nice, gentlemen. Give the lady her cap back. Please." His request held a cutting edge, an underlying threat that was impossible to ignore.

The gang members hesitated, then the one with

her cap tossed it in Sarah's direction. It fell to the sidewalk at her feet.

"Pick it up, punk," the biker ordered, freezing Sarah to the spot before she was able to reach for the cap herself. "Or you're not gonna have any toes left."

Eyeing the biker cautiously, the man did as he was told and carefully handed Sarah her cap.

"Hop on, sweetheart," the biker said, glancing briefly in her direction. The visor shielded his face from view. "I'll take you wherever you want to go."

Through the dreamlike haze, she strained to penetrate the gray plastic mask hiding him, to get even a hint of what he looked like. His voice was so familiar, so strong and determined. He carried himself with such confidence. If only she could see his eyes, she'd know—

"Mama! Mama!"

Sarah bolted to her feet as Becky came running into the living room. Her senses still reeling with strange images—with fear and hope and relief—she caught her daughter in midflight. *Who was the dream man on the motorcycle? He seemed so real. Familiar.*

"What is it, child?" she asked, residual emotions pulsing through her.

"There's a monster under my bed!" Becky's eyes were wide and filled with fear, real or imagined.

"Rebecca Sue, you know you're not to make up wild tales," Sarah admonished.

"But it's true. I heard it. Fannie has to come quick. The monster's sick!" Her mother having rebuked her fear, Becky grabbed the healer's hand, tugging her toward the stairs. "You can fix sick monsters, can't you?"

Fannie met Sarah's gaze and smiled. "Taking care of monsters just happens to be one of my specialties."

Though she should have, Sarah didn't object to their leaving or to Becky's fanciful story. Since Amos had died and the boys had moved out of the house, her daughter had needed extra attention almost as if she were afraid Sarah might vanish, too.

And, if truth be told, what Sarah had just seen—the dream—had left her deeply shaken. The strange images lingered on the fringes of her awareness but she couldn't quite bring them into focus. Fannie's hands had been so soothing, easing the tension from her shoulders, Sarah must have drifted off to sleep for a moment. How terribly rude of her. She'd really have to apologize to her house guest for such inconsiderate behavior.

Sitting down heavily in the rocker again, she covered her face with her hands. What dark, frightening part of her mind had that dream come from? She'd never lived in a town larger than Peacock, and had never been accosted by a gang of ruffians. Or been rescued by a stranger on a motorcycle.

Dear heaven! Why would she even imagine such a thing?

Amos would never have permitted her to go to the city, nor would she have done so on her own.

The thought didn't bear thinking about. Those she had known who challenged the rules set down by the settlement were forever and always shunned. No longer could any relative or friend speak to them; no longer could they even sup at the same table. To be ostracized was the dreadful price to be paid for giving up one's faith.

Sarah would never put herself at risk like that. Or her child.

"Are you all right?"

She lifted her head at the sound of Fannie's voice. A kerosene lantern haloed the healer's features as though she were wearing a bright, plastic helmet, and for a moment the earth seemed to shift on its axis. Sarah's stomach knotted and she blinked, forcing the image away.

"Just tired, I think." She stood, her limbs heavy. "I haven't been a good hostess, and I'm sorry Becky troubled you with her—"

"The monster is sleeping soundly now. So is Becky. A little abracadabra chant did the trick for both of them." Fannie's smile softened the hard angles and planes of her face without making them any less strong. "She's a real little pistol, isn't she?"

Pistol? What an odd expression for someone who must surely be a pacifist, Sarah mused. "My daughter requires a strong hand, which I am far too softhearted to apply. Amos was more firm with her."

"I like that you're softhearted. Women should be. And Becky's just fine as she is. Having an imagination is a gift."

"Do you think so?"

"You bet." In an automatic gesture, Ben tried to stuff his hands into his pockets—and got his hands tangled in his skirt instead. His own imagination was doing a fine job right about now. With little effort, he could imagine removing Sarah's organdy cap and loosening her coiled braids, letting the long strands of her flaxen hair pour through his fingers.

The whole time he had been massaging her neck and shoulders, he'd wanted to do that. And more.

He'd been remembering, that first night they had met. Trying to get from the bus depot to the YWCA, she'd gotten lost on foot in the worst part of town. He'd taken her where she wanted to go, only to discover the Y was closed for remodeling and wouldn't be open again for months. She didn't have much money—and sure couldn't have afforded even a cheap hotel for long. So he'd done the only reasonable thing.

He offered to take her home with him.

He'd seen the anxiety in her eyes at the thought of going to a stranger's apartment, and her courage and determination to succeed in her quest for a nursing education. When she made the decision to go with him, she'd looked at Ben with such faith and purity of spirit, he wouldn't have been able to harm a single hair on her head if his life had depended upon it.

"It is past my bedtime," she said softly, studying him with a tilt to her head. She did that when she puzzled over something she didn't quite understand.

He wondered if she was beginning to remember and hoped so.

"Will you be needing anything before you turn in?" she asked.

Oh, yeah. You in my arms, he thought. "No, I'll be fine, thanks."

"Tomorrow is a church day. You'll join the family, *ja?*"

"Ah, sure." At least it would mean Sarah wouldn't have a chance to question him about herbal remedies.

"Then next week there's a barn raising at Sadie's Joe's, which means I will have to do some baking. I'm not sure when we can get back to my healing lessons. Perhaps after I've done the baking. I hope you don't mind."

Ben stifled a grin. "Hey, there's no hurry. I've got all the time in the world." All the time it took for Sarah to remember him—and their love.

"When it comes time for baking, you're welcome to join me and make up something special of your own to take along."

Ben had pretty well used up his specialties by knocking out that bad old monster under Becky's bed upstairs. "Sure, I'll see what I can whip up." Though he doubted she had a cake mix handy, which would be the only way he'd ever be able to make a cake.

BEN WAS CONVINCED HE was going to die en route to church.

He watched in horror as a big sedan roared up

behind the buggy and, at the very last second, swerved out to pass on the two-lane blacktop road. In the front seat, Sarah and her stepson John seemed unmoved by their near disaster. The well-trained horse didn't so much as flinch.

Whew! And some folks thought motorcycles were dangerous.

"Do you go to church at your house, Fannie?" Becky asked. She was sitting next to him, both of them facing backward, their feet dangling over the edge of the buggy. Dressed in her Sunday best, she was wearing a black bonnet on top of her organdy cap. Ben had been forced to do the same. And he'd been happy to sit in back where Sarah's stepson couldn't get a close look at him. Or use his rifle, if he still had it with him.

"Probably not as often as I ought to," Ben confessed. Which wasn't hardly ever. His folks hadn't exactly been church goers.

"Mama said church is the most 'portant thing in the whole world for Amish folks."

"Yeah, I guess that's right."

"It's hard to sit still so long." Thoughtfully, Becky kicked her legs back and forth, making her skirt flip up to her knobby knees. "Mama says it'll be easier when I gets growed up."

Ben rested his hand on Becky's slender shoulder. "I'm sure it will, Miss Muffet."

She glanced up at him with her big, innocent eyes. "How come you called me that?"

"Haven't you heard of Little Miss Muffet who sat on a tuffet eating her curds and whey?" He grinned at her, surprised at himself because he remembered the nursery rhyme at all. "Along came a spider and sat down beside her, frightening Miss Muffet away."

She giggled, a wonderful sound that wrapped itself right around Ben's heart and held on tight. "I'm not afraid of spiders!"

Lowering his voice, he tickled her in the ribs. "Only afraid of abracadabra monsters, huh?"

Her response was another surge of giggles, so carefree Ben wanted to hug her.

Darn it all! Most of the women he'd met in the past few years had been as much interested in his seven-figure bank account as they were in him. Sarah—and now her daughter—appeared to be perfectly content with what he viewed as simple pleasures.

Glancing over his shoulder, he discovered Sarah looking at him and smiling.

"Are you two all right back there?" she asked.

"We're fine." Better than fine, he thought, realizing it was actually possible to make friends with a little kid.

"If you want to ride up front, I'll change places with you," Sarah offered.

"Fannie wants to stay with me, Mama. We're talkin' 'bout 'portant stuff."

Amusement sparkled in Sarah's eyes. "You behave yourself, you hear me, Rebecca Sue?"

Becky's "Yes, Mama" was nearly swallowed in a giggle.

More than anything, Ben wanted to gather both

Becky and Sarah in his arms and take them away with him. Soon, he told himself. Soon Sarah would remember and be willing to come away with him.

CHURCH SERVICES WERE HELD in one of the homes of the congregation members. The furniture had been removed from both the living and dining rooms, and a wall slid back to create one large room. Benches had been brought in, the women sitting on one side of the hall, the men on the other.

Squirming uncomfortably on the backless bench, Ben wondered how these folks had so many babies when the men and women hardly talked to each other, much less showed any public displays of affection. At first—when he and Sarah had become lovers—she'd been uncomfortable even holding hands with him when they'd been walking down the street. Later, he remembered she'd kissed him once right in front of all his buddies at the construction site. Boy, had they ever hooted and hollered—and been envious as hell.

He glanced at Sarah seated next to him, her hands folded primly in her lap, her daughter sitting on the far side of her. Damn! It was torture not to be able touch Sarah.

On Ben's right, Short Martha was mashed up against him, apparently content to sit like a statue for hours on end. Ben's butt couldn't take it.

As far as he could tell, the sermon had gone on forever. It was hot and airless in the room. Ben's bra was rubbing him raw, and sweat edged down his spine. Wondering what time it was, he auto-

matically glanced at his wrist—his absent watch—
and got no help there. He'd heard these services
typically went on for three hours. This one already
felt like ten.

Slowly, his head tipped forward. A fly buzzed
lazily around the room.

Short Martha's sharp elbow collided with his
ribs.

He nearly jumped out of his skin. "What?" he
hissed.

"You were snoring," she whispered with false
sweetness.

He glowered at her. He *never* snored.

Sarah leaned toward him, lightly brushing her
breast against his upper arm, setting Ben's teeth on
edge as well as certain other parts of his anatomy.
"Becky is restless, *ja?* I'm going to take her to the
kitchen for a snack. Perhaps you would like to
come, too?"

Rescued, at last!

They edged out of the row of benches, leaving
Short Martha and her razor-sharp elbows behind. In
the kitchen he discovered a gaggle of women with
young children and babies in their arms.

"*Ach,* Fannie," one of the women from the quilting bee whispered, mindful of the preacher in the
other room. "My Molly is fussing so. You're a
healer. If you could hold her for a minute…"

The woman thrust the baby into Ben's arms. His
eyes widened. He'd never held a baby. Ever. And
this one was soaking wet! But the kid quieted down

instantly, staring back at him as if she'd never seen such a funny-looking woman in her entire life.

Ben grimaced, trying to keep the baby at arm's length. Ah, hell! There was stuff about being a woman he'd never get right.

Between the quilting bee, these women expecting too much of him, and Short Martha's suspicions, he was lucky he hadn't totally given his masquerade away. And it was too soon to risk that. Somehow he had to ease Sarah toward the truth. If he was unmasked too abruptly, before she'd remembered enough, trusted him enough, she might throw him out of her life entirely.

His last chance would be gone.

CHURCH DAYS WERE LONG and arduous, Sarah mused as she pulled her simple cotton nightgown over her head that evening. Today had been particularly stressful.

For some reason, as the afternoon wore on, she hadn't been able to keep her mind off Fannie, always aware of where the healer was, wanting to make sure that she was comfortable. Time and again, Sarah had told herself that was natural. Fannie was her house guest. Her responsibility.

But her concerns had run deeper than that. Almost possessive.

With a shake of her head, Sarah turned down the light and climbed into bed. Outside, the crickets chirped noisily; inside the house, she could still hear Fannie moving around across the hall.

Through the darkness, Sarah stared at the ceiling above her and listened.

Guilt niggled at her conscience. If truth be told, she'd never enjoyed sharing her marriage bed with Amos. He'd been kind, of course. And a good father. But their matings had been infrequent and hasty, lacking all but the most essential intimacies, and Sarah had always been left feeling empty. Unfulfilled. *Barren.*

With her approaching marriage to Samuel, she wondered if she would experience more of the passion her friends sometimes alluded to. Somehow she thought not.

Restless, she turned on her side, curling into a ball. What would it be like, she wondered, to be aroused by the patient, lingering caress of a man's hands on her body, of his lips kissing her in intimate, secret places.

Her nipples puckered at the thought, her skin heating under the imaginary caress of a stranger. As fragile as the wings of a butterfly, her inventive mind toyed with the possibilities. Heat coiled slowly through her midsection. Her breathing deepened, her chest rising and falling against the crisp cotton sheet, smooth where his hands would be rough with calluses. But gentle. Oh, so gentle.

Her fingers flexed, imagining the feel of his hair bunching in her hands as she pulled his mouth to hers—strands curling like silk to capture her. She tasted the sharp, tangy flavor of the beer he'd drunk; inhaled his musky, uniquely masculine scent, a combination of sawdust and hard work.

Pleasure shivered through her. And anticipation. He drew out the kiss, ever deeper and more demanding, until she could hardly breathe at all.

With him, she opened like a rosebud stroked by the rays of a summer sun. She arched toward his heat. He claimed her breast with his mouth, and she trembled, a sob of delectable pleasure catching in her throat. The elemental need in her ached for release.

He rose above her, a stranger in silhouette. Her lover.

Heedlessly, she raised herself to meet him, the bedsprings squeaking beneath her. Her arms searched for him, finding nothing but empty darkness.

Her eyes flew open. Body still pulsing with need, she breathed in quick, hungry gulps of air. Where had he—

But she was alone; her imaginary lover had deserted her, leaving her alone with her sinful thoughts and loveless bed. Rolling over, she buried her head in her pillow, trying to press the shame of her secret desires away.

It was a long time before her traitorous thoughts allowed her respite in sleep.

THE FOLLOWING MORNING, Ben came downstairs to find Sarah just coming in the back door to the kitchen. She had a basket of eggs hooked over her arm, a shawl around her shoulders, and her face was flushed as though the first rays of sunlight had left their rosy mark.

"Good morning, Fannie," she said brightly. "It's going to be a lovely day."

"It already is." Any morning when Sarah greeted him was a perfect day, he thought as his gaze traveled appreciatively down the length of her body. No dress on earth could entirely conceal the shape of her breasts or the narrowness of her waist above the gentle swell of her hips. She was barefoot, as she loved to be, and her ankles were slender, her feet fine-boned, her toes perfect. A long time ago he'd heard the foot was an erogenous zone, and that if a man caressed a woman's foot just right, she'd become aroused. He'd tried it more than once with Sarah. Whoever had told him that had been right. Of course, once she'd discovered her passionate side, it had never taken her long to become eager for their lovemaking.

For that matter, it never took him long, either, he thought with a satisfied grin.

She placed the egg basket on the kitchen counter. "Daniel came by at first light to say they're needing more quilts at the store. Though our tourists are often a bother, trying to take our pictures and all, it is hard to be upset when they buy our merchandise. It's a good business we have."

Ben wasn't really interested in her quilting business; at the moment, her cute little pink toes held his full attention.

Rinsing her hands under the faucet, she said, "I'll have to be gone for an hour or two. The baking will have to wait, unless—"

He raised his gaze to meet hers.

"I know it's an imposition, Fannie, but would you mind making the cakes for the barn raising?"

"Me?" His high-pitched voice cracked.

"I'd do it, of course. But by the time I return from town, the heat of the day will be on us."

"I'll take your quilts to town and you can—"

"Oh, but I have to gather them up from the other ladies at their homes and then mark and price them. The consignment system is a bit complicated. I thought baking a few cakes would be easier for you."

"That makes sense." Or it would have if he knew anything about baking.

Her smile was radiant with relief. "It's fortunate that you're here, Fannie. Such a help you'll be, watching Becky and doing the baking. I'm ever so grateful to you."

Well, hell. What was a man supposed to do but say yes to a grateful woman who smiled at him like that? He'd give his shirt off his back to help Sarah. She'd always affected him that way. Of course, at the moment, he didn't *have* a shirt. And he didn't imagine he should rip off his bulky dress.

A HALF HOUR LATER, faced with a huge kitchen, two stoves and an array of eggs, spices, sugar, and flour spread out on the counter, Ben did the only thing he could. He enlisted Becky as a partner in crime. The best he could hope for was that a five-year-old raised in an Amish community would know more about making a cake than he did.

''So what do you think we ought to do first?'' he asked innocently.

''We've gots to measure the flour.''

''That's absolutely right, Becky. What a smart little girl you are.''

She beamed a toothy smile in his direction—a smile that when she got older would melt a guy's heart from about five hundred paces. ''My mama taught me.''

Assuming Becky had learned her lessons well, this project would go just fine. ''How much flour do you think we need?'' he asked.

''How many cakes are we going to bake?''

He frowned. ''How many does your mother usually make?''

She held up six fingers. ''One more than I am old,'' she told him.

''Okay, then. Let's do it.''

Measuring and sifting flour didn't appear to be a particularly precise art. It flew all over the tabletop. Sugar did the same. Eggshells were a different matter. More often than not, they fell into the bowls along with the yokes. The whites tended to dribble down the outside of the bowls. When Ben figured they'd lost too much of one egg, he simply had Becky crack another one, most of which went into the mix.

As they worked together, Becky kneeling on a chair beside him, Ben decided they made a good team. He'd never given much thought to having kids, not even when he and Sarah had been living together. Neither of them had seemed ready for that big a step. But now, hanging around with Becky and checking out her cute little face all covered with flour, he didn't think the idea was so bad. In fact, he envied Amos Yoder for having had the chance to know Becky from the beginning.

Chapter Four

"Look what we did, Mama!"

Sarah stood slack jawed in her kitchen—her usually *spotless* kitchen. She'd been gone less than two hours. From all appearances, a tornado had passed through during her absence, covering the place in a fine dusting of flour and leaving behind six of the most lopsided cakes she'd ever seen. At first she thought they were iced with chocolate. Then she realized the cakes were burned black.

She shot Fannie a questioning look. "My gracious, you two have been busy, haven't you?"

The healer grinned at her sheepishly. "We had some trouble adjusting the oven temperature."

"Yes, I can see that."

"Then we got distracted when Becky wanted to show me her dolls. One of the arms had come off."

"I helped Fannie fix it, Mama." Becky's smile was as proud as a peacock.

"That's very nice." Sarah's lips twitched, and she fought for a middle ground somewhere between laughter and dismay.

"Becky thought the cakes would be okay after we put some of your white-mountain icing on them, but we wanted to wait until they cooled off."

Sarah shifted her gaze to her daughter, whose blue dress and bib apron were covered with so much flour the child looked like a snowman.

"Fannie said charcoal is good for us, Mama. It cleans out your innards."

"*Ja?*" She raised a skeptical brow. Fannie's dress hadn't fared much better than Becky's, and the healer's cap looked as though they'd been using it as a flour sifter. "Well, I'm sure everyone at the barn raising will appreciate that."

"Come on, little Miss Muffet," Fannie said to Becky. "Let's see if we can get this place cleaned up for your mom."

"*Ach,* no, why don't you let me do that?" Sarah pleaded somewhat desperately. "After all, it's you two who have done all the hard work by baking the cakes. It's only fair that I do the cleanup."

"If you're sure?" the healer asked.

"Oh, *ja,* very sure." Sarah definitely wanted Fannie out of her kitchen, though she considered it quite odd the woman was so unskilled at baking that she'd permitted this disaster to happen. Her daughter's limitations she could understand, but an adult Amish woman who couldn't cook? Quite peculiar, indeed.

Though the healer had managed to repair Becky's doll, Sarah conceded. A valuable service to the household—one that Amos or his sons had usually performed before her husband's death.

She wasn't sure what to make of Fannie's growing relationship with Becky, either. They'd certainly formed an attachment. Perhaps it was simply that Becky missed her brothers and needed a friend to play with. Fannie seemed willing enough.

"Perhaps after I finish straightening the kitchen, we can pursue my lessons in healing," Sarah suggested.

Even beneath the flour, Fannie's face paled markedly. "Good idea. Absolutely. We'll, ah, get right to it."

With a puzzled frown, Sarah watched as her daughter and the healer escaped out the back door to visit the barn and chicken coop. Fannie had the heaviest footsteps, Sarah mused—almost as if she were used to wearing boots instead of the sturdy oxfords in the style that Sarah wore.

She blinked and the image of heavy work boots popped into her mind—wearing apparel that wasn't at all like that worn by Amish farmers in her community. Certainly no woman Sarah knew would wear shoes like that.

WHILE BECKY WAS PLAYING with a new litter of kittens, Ben slipped out of the barn the back way. He'd spotted a public phone booth at the end of the lane. The Amish didn't have phones in their homes, believing that face-to-face visits were better than what they viewed as impersonal calls; but they weren't averse to using a phone in an emergency. Ben definitely needed help.

He hiked up his skirt, dug into his jeans pocket

and found a quarter. The phone rang three times at the feed store before Seth picked up.

"What do you know about healing?" Ben asked.

There was silence for several heartbeats. "Who is this?"

"It's me. Ben Miller. Sarah's putting the pressure on for me to teach her some healing stuff."

"She hasn't remembered you yet, I gather."

"No." But she was going to. Ben had sensed the other night that she'd remembered *something* just before Becky had come looking for help with her monster. "I've got to play for time, Seth. Give me some tidbit or other that will make me look like I know what I'm doing."

"Far as I know, they make teas and concoctions out of almost anything."

"Could you be a little more specific? *Please.*" He glanced out of the phone booth, a wooden building that looked a lot like an outhouse. Becky could be coming along almost any minute, and he didn't want to get caught making this call. She'd probably blab to her mom, who'd ask questions he wasn't yet ready to answer.

"The wife might know some details but she's not here."

Great! Ben rolled his eyes. He could only fake this healer business so far based on his first aid training. If he gave some bad advice, Sarah might end up killin' somebody.

"Why don't you try using the hands-on approach?" Seth suggested.

"Huh?"

"I've heard Amish healers use touch in their faith healing, along with some chiropractic manipulations. Seems to me, son, you *touching* Forgetful Sarah just might help cure her memory loss."

An excuse to touch Sarah again? Oh, yeah, he liked that idea. And the other night he could have sworn—

He spotted Becky trotting down the lane.

"Gotta go, Seth. Thanks a lot."

Ben had barely gotten his skirt straightened—at the cost of another pin jammed in his midsection—when Becky arrived at his side. A tiny yellow kitten was tucked up by her chin, and she slid her free hand into his.

"Want me to show you around the neighborhood?" she asked brightly. "I know just 'bout everybody there is."

"I bet you do." Slightly awed by the child's trusting ways, Ben allowed her to lead him alongside the blacktop road. "Should we tell your mother we're going for a walk?"

"It's okay. She says I can go as far as Hosettler's house, but *no* further 'less I'm with somebody else."

Ben wasn't sure if he qualified as "somebody else" or not, but Becky seemed confident they weren't violating any house rule.

"My brother John keeps his car behind Hosettler's barn but I'm not s'posed to tell anybody that."

"Then I won't mention you said anything."

"It's real comp'cated to be Amish." Cuddling

the kitten, she glanced up at Ben. "See, the Hosettler's are outsiders, so it's okay if they have a car.
But it's not okay for us."

"So John has to keep his car a secret."

She nodded solemnly. "'Cept everybody knows.
They just don't say so."

"That does seem to make things complicated,"
he agreed.

"Mama says I'll understand better when I get
growed-up."

Squeezing her hand, he said, "Your mama is
probably right."

They reached the fence marking the beginning of
the next farm, one that was as equally well kept as
those belonging to Amish families, but with a tractor parked in front of the barn and a pickup in the
driveway. Electric power and phone lines strung
from the poles on the road to the house connected
the Hosettler family to the rest of the world in ways
the Amish wouldn't permit for their own.

"Mama says this is far-calling distance." The
child glanced back at her house, still easily visible
beyond the cornfield that was close to being ready
to harvest. "In case she wants me, this is as far as
she can holler."

"Then I guess we'd better go back, huh?"

She nodded. "Guess so. 'Sides, the kitty probably wants her mama, too."

Reversing direction, Ben was struck by how
peaceful Becky's neighborhood was. In Philadelphia, a mother wouldn't dare let a five-year-old this
far out of sight. Within reason, Sarah seemed quite

comfortable with the idea of her child being on a long leash. After all, there was little traffic and almost no strangers who passed this way.

Except Ben. And he wasn't exactly a stranger.

He just knew who he'd like to be, and that was Sarah's husband. And Becky's dad, he realized with a start.

IN THE HEAT OF THE DAY, they sat in the shade of the front porch. Sarah had made another pitcher of lemonade, and she waited eagerly for the healer to share her knowledge with her. Nearby, a bee was busily harvesting pollen from a bed of daisies and nasturtiums, and the sweet scent of honeysuckle hung in the air.

"Okay, let's start with warts," Fannie said.

Sarah's head snapped around. "Warts?"

"Something simple." Before Sarah could object, Fannie took her hand. "Let's say you've got a wart on your hand, right here on your finger."

"All right," Sarah said hesitantly. Warts weren't exactly high on her priority list for cures, but she supposed she'd have to gain Fannie's trust before the healer would share her more sophisticated methods. Sarah intended to be a good student. When sickness could strike a community so suddenly, and at such great cost, she wanted to be ready to help.

"Now, there's lots of poultices you could use, right?"

"Yes," she responded. Some of the home cures were quite successful when it came to warts.

"But in a person's touch there's the power of healing, too."

Sarah believed that was true because the feel of Fannie's hand on hers seemed to carry a warm, electric charge. They were big hands, working hands with square-cut nails, and the friction of them triggered a response in her nerve endings clear up her arm.

"If you rub long enough…" The healer's thumb skimmed over Sarah's hand again and again, shifting across the back and then sliding to the sensitive center of her palm to circle there—lingering warmly. "A person's circulation speeds up."

"Yes," she said, her breathing accelerating along with the flow of her blood. "I can feel it. You have an amazing power, Fannie." A power that was erotic in its potency. The healer's hands were broad and roughened with calluses compared to her own. Sarah could only imagine how much hard work the woman had performed to have lost every bit of softness in her hands. But they were still gentle.

"Letting your patient know she—or he—is safe with you is important. You're safe with me, Sarah. You always will be."

Light-blue eyes touched hers with more intensity than a simple glance. They probed her, penetrated her defenses, demanding a response Sarah didn't know how to give.

"I'm not afraid," Sarah responded, searching for the answer Fannie seemed to want.

"I never want you to be afraid. Not with me."

The image of prowling hooligans flashed into her

mind along with the sense of safety nearby. She reached for that security and found she was squeezing Fannie's hand.

She gasped. "I'm sorry... I thought—"

"It's all right, Sarah. You're learning to trust me. These things take time."

"It's important for me to learn—" A sob caught in her throat, a crack forming in the dam of emotions she struggled to keep in check. "I was the oldest girl in my family. There were four younger than I, four so helpless, two girls and two little boys. It was diphtheria that took them. My parents—"

Her head pounded. She'd only been ten at the time. In Fannie's eyes she saw understanding as she spoke of the guilt, the burden of anguish she'd secretly carried for so long. She'd wanted to run away, as if by doing that she could somehow turn back the clock. Find a way to save her brothers and sisters. Or others like them. She'd become an outsider, if that was what it took. But her parents had said no; they had no need for a worldly daughter. They'd frightened her. *Shamed* her for her thoughts. Her dreams. Made less of her remorse. "If they had only believed in immunizations, the babies might have—"

"I know, sweet Sarah. It wasn't your fault."

"But I have to find ways to help other babies. They shouldn't die. It isn't fair."

Suddenly she felt Fannie's arms around her and they felt like the arms of another. Strong. Powerful. Capable of sustaining her when all else had failed.

Tears poured down her cheeks, dampening the healer's shawl. Sarah fought against the wrenching sobs that racked her body. When had she last cried like this? So many years ago the memory was little more than smoke. But the arms, the musky scent of the one who held her—

With a start, she shoved back from Fannie.

"Who are you?" she demanded.

"Someone who is here to help you heal."

"I'm not sick. It is I who wants to help others."

"I understand that, Sarah. God help me, I know you have a gift that few others possess. I want to help you achieve your dream. I want to be a part of it."

Sarah stared at this stranger who had come into her home. Who was this healer who could touch her in ways she'd never before imagined? Or perhaps she had dreamed of these feelings in the darkest part of the night when she was alone with her own secrets.

Secrets that teased at the edge of her awareness; images that, once remembered, would change her life forever and leave her without hope of redemption.

Snatching her hand back from Fannie, she leaped to her feet. Warmth flushed her face like a summer heat wave. "Enough lessons for today, Fannie. I've still work to do for the barn raising on the morrow."

A SLEEPLESS NIGHT DROVE Sarah from her bed early the next morning, eager to have her chores done before for the barn raising.

Just as she was leaving, Becky and Fannie already in the buggy and waiting, she checked the upstairs to be sure her daughter had left her room in order. Finding nothing amiss, she glanced into the bathroom, whose door stood ajar. Amos had been rightfully proud of the modern facility he'd constructed, though he had tried to remain humble.

She frowned, finding it odd that the toilet seat had been left up. That hadn't happened since the boys had moved out of the house and Amos had been called by his Maker. Becky certainly wouldn't have been so careless.

A renewed prickle of unease edged down Sarah's spine. Between her troubling dreams and the odd feelings she'd gotten around Fannie, something very peculiar was going on here. Sarah would have to be on her guard.

"HEP, HEP." THE ACTING foreman called the cadence as a cadre of workers raised the frame by hand for a section of the barn. Others used spike poles with nails on the ends, jabbing them firmly into the wood to lift it higher until the section was finally vertical and the segment was settled into place. In practiced moves, men tied ropes to the top to steady it while others nailed braces to the floor, everyone working like a well-trained construction crew.

Meanwhile, the sound of doors being constructed

and siding fastened to existing framing echoed across the farmland.

More than three hundred men were hard at work, and Ben's fingers itched to pick up a hammer and join in the fun. Instead he was stuck hanging around with the women, who were discussing the latest recipe for fried chicken and dumplings. Meanwhile, because he'd been talking like a soprano all morning, his throat felt like somebody had taken sandpaper to it.

Edging away from the clutch of women, he hissed out a breath. He wasn't sure how much longer he could maintain this masquerade, or how much longer he'd want to. His head itched from wearing the dumb little cap. Beneath the heavy dress with its long sleeves, his whole body felt chafed. And his bra straps were driving him nutso. Right at the moment, he'd like nothing better than to go skinny-dipping in the farm pond. That would knock the good-hearted friendliness out of all these nice folks, he imagined.

At the far side of the house, the buggies were parked in neat rows, the sleek horses grazing in a nearby field. Ben would have given his soul for a chance to hop on his bike and put a little distance between him and this pretense. Except that when he left, he wanted to take Sarah with him. And Becky, too.

"The cakes you baked look delicious, Fannie."

His head whipped around—and down to Martha. "Well, yes, Becky was a big help."

The little woman's eyes sparkled as though she

knew his secret but wasn't going to tell—yet. "I would not have thought you had such talent. They say nowadays on the outside there are some men who actually do the cooking for their families. Househusbands, they call them."

"I wouldn't know about that," he muttered, hoping he sounded convincing. Though he'd been known to whip up some pretty good spaghetti and a decent omelet now and then. That didn't make him less of a man. But baking cakes was definitely out of his league.

"Perhaps we should recommend to our elders that such a policy be implemented among our people, too."

He glanced around at the men in the work crew, all of whom wore long beards and sported summer straw hats with wide brims. "I don't think you'll get many votes for that one, Martha."

She cackled merrily. "Perhaps you are right, Fannie. But even an Amish woman can have her dreams."

"I suppose."

Her eyes turned serious and a frown pleated her broad forehead. "Some say Forgetful Sarah once had her dreams, but as you are new here, you'd not know about that."

"I might," he said cautiously.

She touched his hand. "Be careful, Fannie. These last few years, Sarah has been content with her child and husband. These are her people. To leave them would be very difficult for her. A second time, she might not be able to return. Nor would her child.''

''It's possible they could both be happy somewhere else.''

''Possible,'' she agreed. ''It's also possible she could be happy remaining here as Samuel's wife. Most Amish women would be. I know I would.''

With that, Martha wandered away, her short legs giving her an awkward gait. She'd also given Ben something to think about—in addition to why the hell she hadn't blown the whistle on him yet.

He glanced around, spotting Sarah with a group of her friends setting up for lunch under a tent on the sprawling lawn that fronted the farmhouse. Children too young to help played tag on the grass, laughing and sometimes fleeing to the safety of their mothers' skirts before they got caught.

Ben had never had anything that resembled a family, and his folks sure had never had anyone they could call friends—except the derelicts they drank with at the local bar. He couldn't remember ever going on a family picnic or having relatives over for dinner.

Whereas the closeness of family and friends were an everyday part of Sarah's life. And of Becky's, too.

Did he have a right to take them both away from all that was familiar to them? Never for a minute did he think Sarah would leave without her child; he wouldn't want her to.

Like a hangnail, he worried the thought.

Sure, Sarah had once wanted to be a nurse so

badly that she'd left the comfort of her Amish community. She'd rebelled. Her guilt over the unnecessary deaths of her younger siblings had driven her to seek an education so she could be a public-health nurse. But she'd been only eighteen at the time. Since then, she could have changed her mind.

She could have changed her mind about Ben, too.

There was no guarantee that even if she remembered him she would still love him. On the outside, his newly acquired wealth could buy him a lot of things. But not here. Not Sarah.

His stomach knotted. The noise from the construction site throbbed in his head, and he rubbed his hand across the back of his neck.

Dammit all! He loved Sarah. With her, he'd caught a glimpse of the life he'd wanted and never thought he'd have. Or deserved. They'd gone on winter picnics in the park together, and she'd invited her friends over for dinner—though his apartment couldn't handle but one other couple at a time. She'd made him invite his friends too, the guys and their wives from his construction job. And his boss, who was now his partner, Mac Culdane, a man who'd become more like a father to him than the one whom Ben had called Dad.

Sarah had wanted the sense of family and friends around her, Ben realized. She'd wanted to re-create, in some small way, what she had left behind. Forever.

However much he had tried, had wanted to be, *he* hadn't been enough for her. That realization rattled him as if he'd taken a first-class punch to his jaw.

Maybe it was asking too much of Sarah to expect her to give all of this up for him.

A man about sixty with a gray beard that grew to his belt buckle sauntered up the rise to where Ben was standing beneath an elm. Tugging self-consciously on the strings of his cap, Ben tried to shake his unsettled feelings aside.

"Heard you were the healer from Plymouth," he said, looking off toward the barn. "Got me some trouble with passing water. Thought you might have some say so what would help."

Ben's lips twitched. Now this was a problem he knew something about—not like the "women's troubles" they'd wanted him to solve. Ben's father had had prostate problems and had tried every half-baked cure he could think of—anything to avoid surgery except giving up his booze.

"Might try the berries of the saw palmetto," Ben suggested, feeling confident for the first time since he'd decided to be a "healer." "You can't raise them here but they do down in Florida. Might be a health-food store in Peacock where you could get some."

"That a fact?"

"That's what I've heard."

The older man scratched at his beard. "Been thinking the problem might be I haven't had a woman in a while. Been thinking I might marry again." He turned and grinned at Ben. "You be a single lady?"

A coughing attack caught Ben so hard he nearly choked. "Not exactly," he managed to say, gulping for breath.

"Pity." The old codger gave him the once-over, slow and lazy like. "Fine-looking woman, you are. I like 'em big and strong. You could be a big help, come harvesting time."

The heat that flamed Ben's cheeks was like the flare of the sun. Oh, man, he really couldn't do this. Some old coot who was half blind was hitting on him? He'd about reached his limit with this masquerade business.

"You and me could take in a Sunday-night singing with the young folks," the old man suggested.

"I don't think so." Not in this lifetime.

"Then I could stop by Forgetful Sarah's place where you're staying late some night." He waggled his shaggy gray eyebrows. "Used to be I enjoyed a bit of bundling when I was a youngster. Could be you did, too?"

Ben sidestepped away. "I gotta go help with lunch," he mumbled, escaping as quickly as he could. He ought to just tell Sarah who he was and why he was there—and do it when he was wearing something decent, for God's sake. Like jeans and a T-shirt. Or one of his five-hundred-dollar Armani suits.

Becky intercepted him before he reached the lunch tent.

"How come you was talkin' to Dirty Peter?" she asked.

"*Dirty* Peter?"

"I heard one of Mama's friends say he was a dirty old man, but he seems clean enough to me."

"Trust me, Little Miss Muffet, your mama's friend is right on. And you keep clear of him, you hear?" Ben intended to do the same. Hell, if the guys in Philadelphia *ever* got wind of this fiasco...

They skirted the food area and went around to the far side of the barn to take a look at the progress. The structure was going up with amazing speed. As a contractor, Ben would give his right arm—and maybe a bonus—to have a crew that worked so hard and so carefully.

"How come girls don't get to hammer and saw?" Becky asked. She was gazing with interest at the men working on the roof, hammering sheets of tin over the framing, her head tilted at the same endearing angle her mother used when puzzling over something she didn't understand.

"There's no reason why a girl can't use a hammer and saw," he said.

She blinked up at him. "Do you know how?"

"Sure I do. It's not all that hard."

"Would you teach me?"

"Maybe when you're older."

She glanced up at the barn-in-progress and then back to Ben. "I want to learn now." There was another look in her eye—a determined one that also mimicked her mother's stubbornness. Ben had learned a long time ago he couldn't fight that.

"Okay, you got a hammer and nails?"

As if she'd been waiting for the signal, she shot

off. Ten seconds later she was back with her prize hammer and a fistful of nails.

"Where'd you find the hammer?" he asked.

"Nobody was using it. They're eating lunch."

"Hmm. Well, I guess it's okay. But we'll have to give it back."

She gave two or three quick nods. "I'm ready."

Looking around for some scrap wood to practice on, Ben had to suppress a smile. Becky had to be the most eager apprentice carpenter he'd ever met.

He gathered up a few pieces of wood and placed them on the ground, a one-by-six plank about a foot long across a couple of two-by-fours.

"Can't I work on the roof?"

"Not yet, Miss Muffet. You've gotta practice first at ground level." He sure wasn't going to be responsible for the kid falling off the roof. And she'd be up there in a flash if he gave the word.

She eased down next to him as he instructed her in the fine art of embedding a nail in a piece of wood without smashing a thumb or bending the head. Her forehead puckered in concentration. Becky was definitely going to be a heartbreaker.

"What in blue blazes are you doing with my hammer, Rebecca Sue?"

The child jumped up as if she'd been goosed, her wide eyes going to the man standing before them. "Fannie's teaching me to hammer."

"No little Amish girl needs to know such a thing."

The stranger snatched the hammer from Becky, then directed his scowl at Ben. "Her menfolk will take care of any hammering she needs doing.'' He was a tall man, his body lean, and the part of his face not covered by a beard was weathered by the sun. A farmer. A man who was butting into Ben's business.

''If Becky wants to learn to use a hammer, I say good for her. Girls can do anything they damn well please these days.'' The child burrowed into Ben's skirts to hide herself. Instinctively, he looped his arm across her narrow shoulders.

''I'm Samuel Mast and soon I will marry the child's mother.'' He knelt in front of Beckly. ''You're a fine girl and you'll make me proud when I am your pa, won't you Becky?''

''Yes, Samuel,'' the girl said meekly.

Jealousy punched Ben in the gut. His fists clenched. This man was planning to marry his Sarah.

Almost as bad, he was planning to limit Becky, telling her what she could or couldn't do. She was too smart to be stuck in a predetermined role before she even had a chance to choose for herself. Besides, if she was smart enough and worked hard enough, she could own her own construction business—just like Ben.

In two strides, unresonable jealousy driving him, Ben narrowed the distance between him and the man who would take choice away from a child. If Ben was being billed as a healer, he figured he had a powerful card to play. One that would make the man squirm.

''Samuel Mast, you do not look well. I see yellow in your eyes. Your complexion is flushed." He shook his head. "How long have you been ill?"

His gaze darted from side to side. "I'm well enough."

"But your stomach. Is that not a problem? And your spleen?"

"You can tell by looking—"

"I'm a healer, Samuel Mast. I know these things." Ben narrowed his gaze, knowing full well Samuel was about to become putty in his hands— the same way bankers folded when he threatened to take his business elsewhere. "Bed rest and rhubarb, lots of it. Prunes would help, too."

"Prunes?"

"It's that serious. If you haven't got any at home, I'd go to town immediately, if I were you. There's no time to waste."

"But I'll be all right, won't I?" A touch of panic darkened Samuel's eyes.

"Only if you do as I say." And stay miles away from my Sarah. And Becky, too.

"I'll do it, of course." He backed up a few steps. "You won't tell Sarah, I trust."

Ben shook his head.

"My children need a mother. Sarah will be good for them. And a helper for me. I would not want her to change her mind about our marriage. She's a fine woman—"

"Yeah, right. Why don't you get on out of here?" Ben demanded, his throat tight at the thought of Sarah marrying this guy—marrying anybody but him. "And take an extra dose of Ex-Lax," he muttered under his breath.

As Samuel hurried away, Ben felt Becky's hand slide into his again.

"What is Ex-Lax?" she asked innocently, her head tipped way back to look up at him, her little white cap cockeyed.

He hefted her into his arms and kissed her cheek. "You don't want to know, Miss Muffet. And don't you dare let *anybody* tell you you can't be a carpenter if that's what you want to be." *Even if Samuel ends up as your old man,* he left unsaid.

Hugging him, she kissed him back, and Ben figured he'd be the luckiest guy in the world to have a little girl like Becky.

Dear God, he couldn't believe Sarah was planning to marry Samuel, and jealousy ate Ben. Samuel couldn't love her—not they way Ben did. But the guy was a part of her community. He was a farmer; Ben was a construction worker through and through, one who finally had plenty of change in his jeans. He could offer a woman more now than the tiny walk-up apartment he'd once shared with Sarah. Not that she'd ever complained.

He squeezed Becky again, mentally resisting the possibility that Sarah might actually *love* Samuel with his dark beard and dour expression. She was too happy a person, too sweet to fall for a grump who didn't know his spleen from his big toe.

"You're squishing me, Fannie," Becky complained. "And making my tummy hurt."

"I am?" Easing his grip, he tickled the tummy in question. "Maybe it's just hungry for lunch."

She giggled and squirmed to get down.

"Okay, Miss Muffet. Let's go find your mama."

Chapter Five

Sarah stood in the shade of the food tent, checking to see that all was in order—including the cakes she'd baked in the wee hours of the morning to replace the dreadful ones made by her daughter and Fannie. Smiling at the memory, Sarah knew, unless pressed, she would never offend the healer by letting her know where her baking efforts had ended up.

By now the men were beginning to drift toward the food tent for their noon meal. Soon the evidence of the missing cakes would be gone.

"Are you enjoying having the healer in your home?"

Turning, Sarah greeted her friend Mona Lutz. Tall and slender, Mona had carrot-red hair and a pleasant disposition, both of which she had passed on to all six of her children.

"*Ach, ja,* Fannie is a fine woman." Though thus far Sarah had learned little of the healing arts, and that troubled her.

"She's a big woman, *ja?*"

With a nod, Sarah let the comment pass without adding that Fannie's features were also amazingly masculine for a woman. So was the way she moved—more athletic than graceful. And sometimes, well… Sarah had the oddest feeling that one of Fannie's breasts sat much higher on her chest than the other, a tragic genetic deformity, she guessed.

"You heard about Jenny's babies, *ja?*"

"*Nein*. What happened?" Sarah hadn't seen Jenny this morning but had been too busy to notice or worry about her friend's absence.

"Her husband came for them this morning at dawn."

"But he left the settlement." It had been weeks since Jenny's husband Michael had moved away to become an outsider. There had been no farmland for him and he'd wanted a worldly life with a job and car, foolish things that would take him away from the community. In much the same way, Sarah had once foolishly coveted an education that was only available on the outside.

"*Ja*, and Jenny wouldn't go with him. So this morning he came with the sheriff and a court order for the children, they say. He's to have custody of them."

"All three? They're little more than babies." Sarah's heart constricted. She could imagine no pain greater than losing Becky. "But she'll get them back, won't she? Even among the outsiders, a mother must have—"

"The bishop is talking with the sheriff but they

say it's out of his hands. She may have to choose between going with Michael or losing her children.''

''But that's awful. No mother could choose—''

''We'd be forced to shun her if she goes with Michael,'' Mona said sadly, shaking her head. ''And the children, too.''

''That's so unfair.'' It was one of the tenets of her church that had always struck Sarah as much too cruel.

''Glad I am my husband has no thought of leaving the settlement.''

''Your husband may someday be chosen as a preacher, so you've no fear of losing your children to the outsiders' foolish laws.''

Nor did Sarah have to fear such a thing. With Amos gone, Becky was hers and hers alone, and would be even after her marriage to Samuel. It was just as well, for the mere thought of leaving her Amish home and friends sent a shiver of apprehension down Sarah's spine. Deep down, the prospect of living in the outside world terrified her as though some ghoulish ghost from the past were knocking on her door.

She'd never have the courage to leave. *Again*, came the errant thought, and she frowned. Where in the world had that come from?

She glanced up to see Fannie walking toward her across the yard. A healer Sarah would be—a mother to Samuel's children—and perhaps there would be more babies for her. Her life would be full, indeed, and she would retain the approval of both her parents, who lived in an Amish community thirty miles north of Peacock.

She cocked her head as Fannie approached. The way the sun slanted off Fannie's broad shoulders and the way she held her head reminded Sarah of someone else. An odd thrill of excitement fluttered in her stomach and tightened her throat—a sexual thrill, as though a phantom lover had come to rescue her by slaying dragons and would soon sweep her away in his arms.

What a strange, fanciful image, she thought with an embarrassed smile.

BEN'S EMPTY STOMACH rumbled as he reached Sarah's side, his innards complaining loudly that it had been a long time since breakfast. She was smiling one of her gentle, heartwrenching smiles and politely looked away while his stomach continued to make its wishes known. Fortunately there was no one else standing nearby to witness his small breach in etiquette.

Tables piled high with fried chicken, dumplings, coleslaw, corn on the cob and rolls were spread out beneath the tent covering. Taking turns, men came off the construction job and filled their plates, finding seats on church pews that had been brought along for that purpose. Meanwhile, the women and children waited.

Not exactly gentlemen, these Amish menfolk, Ben mentally muttered.

His gaze slid to the dessert table. ''Where'd the cakes go that Becky and I baked?'' he asked.

"Perhaps the earliest arrivals ate them all," Sarah said, her expression just a little too innocent.

"Really?" Now that surprised the heck out of him. The Amish must all be martyrs at heart if they passed up a dozen terrific-looking cakes and pies to eat the disasters he and Becky had made. "Guess the icing made the difference, huh?"

Sarah flushed slightly. "It's a very good recipe."

"Hey, you." Suspicious, he caught her chin between his thumb and forefinger. No one was paying them any particular attention and a "healer" was freer than most to touch in ways that might be considered intimate for others. "You wouldn't be lying, now would you?"

"Lying?" She had beautiful blue eyes—honest eyes that revealed her every thought.

"Yeah. What'd you do? Dump them?"

Her blush deepened and Ben became aware of just how soft her skin was, as caressable as a fresh peach. "The Hosettlers' pigs found them very tasty."

He chuckled, and ran his thumb across her lower lip. Now *that* was what he'd find tasty—her sweet, succulent lips—if he were given a chance. She drew a quick breath, and he pulled his hand away. "Why didn't you tell me?" His voice had lowered with the need that thrummed through his body, his falsetto vanishing as his desire rose.

"I did not wish to embarrass you, Fannie."

"But that meant you didn't have anything to bring to this potluck affair."

Her eyebrows rose slightly. "I awakened early this morning and did some more baking."

He'd doubled her work by messing up the cakes but she hadn't complained. Not a word. That was like her.

He remembered one night when he'd tracked in mud right after she'd cleaned the floor. She hadn't complained. But later, after they'd made love and he'd fallen asleep, he'd awakened to hear her scrubbing the floor all over again. She'd been embarrassed when he'd caught her, and pleased when he'd gotten down on his hands and knees to finish the job with her. An Amish man, she'd told him, would not have done such a thing.

And then they'd made love again. She'd always been so ready for him, as though she'd been afraid each time would be their last. He'd half-suspected she'd overcome her resistance to making love before marriage because she missed her family and friends so much. Ben was all she had—all she needed, she'd assured him. They'd been so deeply in love... Then one day she was gone, and he'd begun his search for her.

He drew a deep breath at the memory and his vision blurred. God, he wanted her back.

"What's wrong, Fannie?"

"Nothing." Swallowing, he tried to blink the moisture from his eyes. "It's just that if I'd known, I would have come downstairs to help you."

Sarah palmed the healer's cheek, which felt oddly rough beneath her hand. "You are sweet to offer, Fannie. But I think when it comes to baking cakes, it's better that I do the work myself.''

''Maybe you're right.'' The healer's voice was low, almost intimate, and a shudder sped down Sarah's spine as it had when Fannie had touched her lips a moment ago.

What a strange reaction she had to the woman, almost as if—

But no, she wouldn't give words to the thought. She'd been a married woman and would be again after the harvest was in. But Fannie's eyes were such a striking blue, so light they were almost hypnotizing, and Sarah found herself gazing deeply into them, hoping to find what she didn't know.

She had many women friends here in the community. Their daily lives were much the same as hers, cooking and cleaning and raising their families, and when the season was right, helping during harvest. Visiting and exchanging thoughts about their personal lives was second nature among the women—up to a point. But in Fannie's eyes she saw evidence of a person to whom she could tell everything—even her deepest, darkest secret; private thoughts she would never reveal to anyone else.

There are days when I am not happy with my life. I did not enjoy lying with my husband and did it only out of duty with and the hope that God would bless me with more children. Becky is the most important thing in the world to me. She is growing so fast, I'm afraid that all too soon she will be gone and I will be alone. Can you hear me, Fannie? Would you understand?

Sometimes I dream, and I don't know where those dreams come from, or the voice of the man who is in them.

She blinked and licked her lips. The flow of conversation around her returned as if she'd been away a long time and had only now found her way back to reality.

Becky slipped up beside her, wrapping her arms around Sarah's hips. "Mama, I don't feel good."

Automatically, Sarah felt her daughter's forehead, finding it slightly warm to the touch. "What bothers you, child?"

Becky shrugged. "My tummy hurts."

"What's up?" Fannie asked, concern lowering her brows.

"Too much sun, perhaps," Sarah suggested, not terribly worried at the moment. Becky ran a slight temperature for the least little reason, and the fever would often be gone before Sarah even had a chance to give her a dose of curative tea. Some children were like that, she'd been told. "Or maybe she's coming down with a summer cold."

"Should we do something?" Fannie asked. "I mean, does she need a doctor or something?"

Shaking her head, Sarah smiled. "I imagine she will not need the services of a healer just yet."

Before Fannie had a chance to respond, shouts came from the barn construction site.

"A boy's fallen!"

"He's hurt!"

"His leg, it's ripped open!"

"Get help."

"Get the *healer!*"

Sarah's gaze snapped back to Fannie. Thank goodness a skilled healer was here to aid the injured child.

IT TOOK BEN A FULL THIRTY seconds before he reacted. They wanted him to help the injured youngster. Every eye in the place was on him.

Well, hell!

With no other choice, he hiked up his skirt and broke into a trot across the yard toward the barn. As soon as he reached the fallen youngster, he began to sweat.

The kid had caught himself on the protruding nails of a two-by-four, sliding down the length of the damn board, ripping open his leg in a ten-inch-long gash.

Blood was everywhere.

Gushing.

It covered the boy's dark pants and soaked the ground where he lay, his leg turned awkwardly to the side. His eyes were wide and scared. His chin quivered.

In seventeen years of construction work, Ben had seen his share of accidents. He knew first aid and this kind of emergency was all too common at construction sites.

Acting on experience, he squatted beside the boy, his fool skirts billowing around his legs, and he tore the boy's pant leg open from cuff to groin. He closed his hands over the gash, pressing the edges of the wound together.

"Somebody get an ambulance," he ordered. "And get it here damn quick."

There was movement behind him. Murmuring. But Ben concentrated on stanching the flow of blood. The youngster was maybe fourteen with the build of a soccer player, quick and fast. But if help didn't come in a hurry, he would never run again. He'd be in a handmade pine box six feet under the ground.

"Rest easy, son," he said, trying to calm the boy. "The medics will be here soon. Just lie still."

The boy nodded and fought the tears that were threatening to spill down his pale cheeks.

Ben kept the pressure on the wound. "What's your name, kid?"

"Henry. Henry Yoder." The boy's Adam's apple bounced as he swallowed hard. "You're the healer? Am I goin to—"

"You'll be fine," Ben assured the boy, praying it wasn't a lie.

An Amish woman, who could have been anywhere from thirty to fifty years old, slipped up beside Ben and knelt by the boy. Probably his mother. She smoothed Henry's dark hair off his forehead then lifted her gaze to Ben.

"Thank the good Lord you're here, Fannie," she whispered, her eyes filled with more faith than Ben deserved. *"Danke."*

Ben was glad he knew enough to handle the situation—temporarily. He just wished the ambulance would show up. His hands were sticky with blood, and if the boy didn't receive medical attention soon, he might suffer permanent damage.

He figured by now somebody had made it to the phone out on the main road, either running or in a buggy, and the paramedics should be on their way. His legs throbbed from his awkward squatting position, his fingers cramped, and sweat crept down his face and pooled under his arms. But he didn't let go. Around him, the crowd of onlookers stood in hushed silence. Praying, maybe. He didn't know. He simply held on.

A cool cloth touched his forehead and he looked up. Sarah looked down at him with the same kind of faith that shone in the boy's mother's eyes.

Ben didn't deserve any special treatment. He was simply doing the best he could based on his own experience and the training he'd had.

Finally, after what seemed like an eternity, he heard the approaching siren. The crowd parted.

"I got it, lady." The experienced hands of a paramedic eased him aside.

Staggering to his feet, Ben stepped back to let the men do their job. Sarah hooked her arm through his, steadying him, and it felt good to have her that close, to smell her fresh herbal scent. To know that someone who knew about medicine had taken charge of the boy.

The ambulance crew worked quickly, controlling the bleeding, checking the boy's vital signs, and lifting him onto a stretcher. Henry's mother hovered nearby, and his siblings formed a protective ring around him. His hands clasped in front of him, the boy's father stood stoically to one side.

When the boy was lifted into the ambulance, the crowd let out a collective sigh, and so did Ben. People moved again. The boy's mother and father got into the vehicle with the youngster; other relatives sorted themselves out, making arrangements to follow the ambulance into town in their buggies.

As the ambulance edged away from the half-completed barn, the crowd dispersed, most of the men returning to their work, though now far more subdued than they had been earlier.

"You'll want to wash up, *ja?*" Sarah said, guiding Fannie toward the big farmhouse.

As they passed through the crowd of onlookers, a woman touched Fannie lightly on her arm. *"Danke,"* she whispered, thanking him. Another woman did the same, and a man touched the brim of his straw hat in salute. Sarah's heart filled with reflected pride and another feeling she couldn't identify.

"They're making me into some kind of a hero," Fannie muttered. "I didn't do anything somebody else couldn't have handled. I feel like a fraud."

"You have the hands of a healer, Fannie. We're grateful you were here to help Henry Yoder." As they reached the porch, Sarah drew a deep breath. Like the others, she'd been awed by Fannie's presence, her skill and quiet assurance.

She'd watched the healer's hands in fascination, struck once again by how familiar they looked. It was almost as if she could see—and feel—those same big hands on her. And somehow she knew the hands she imagined were not those of a woman.

At the thought, her breath caught in her chest. What man could she be thinking of? Not Amos, her husband, whose fingers had already been twisted by arthritis when they married. And certainly not Samuel, who had yet to touch her in even the most innocent of ways.

Shaken by her confusion, she held more tightly to Fannie's arm. There was something terribly incongruous about the healer's size, her delicate white cap and her big, gentle hands. Something out of sync. Something Sarah ought to know.

"What's wrong, Sarah?"

"Nothing," she said too quickly. Her head throbbed and she felt dizzy, as though she were standing at the edge of a high cliff and was about to fall off as the boy had fallen from the barn roof. Would Fannie catch her? she wondered. Would the healer's powerful arms hold her safe from harm?

She tried to shake the thought aside, but the image lingered.

The screen door opened. Naomi Lapp welcomed them inside, and Sarah was forced to release her grip on Fannie's arm. Soon other women followed them into the house. Sarah stood aside, her heart heavy, her mind troubled, watching as her friends sang the healer's praises.

The toilet seat in the bathroom Fannie used had been left up that morning. The first time since the boys had moved out. *Fannie's breasts were uneven, as though deformed. Or false. And more than once, a curse had slipped from Fannie's lips.* Words an Amish woman wouldn't say.

In the four short days that Fannie had been staying at Sarah's farm, she'd increasingly felt something was very wrong. Now she was nearly sure of it.

IT WAS LATE BY THE TIME they left the Lapp farm after the barn raising. Becky curled up in Fannie's lap for the buggy ride home, and Sarah remained thoughtful. Once she had her daughter in bed, she had questions to ask of the healer—if indeed that's who Fannie was.

But who else? Had the woman not demonstrated her skill that very afternoon? And come to Peacock, to Sarah's house, with an impeccable reputation?

Images of another time, another place, tormented Sarah but they wouldn't come into focus.

At the house, they all went upstairs, Sarah taking Becky to her room and helping her to change out of her dress and into her nightgown. The child's face looked flushed. She was unusually subdued as she crawled into her bed and curled into a ball.

"My tummy still hurts, Mama," she complained.

Her fever had risen, the child's forehead no longer warm but hot to the touch, and she'd eaten no dinner at all. "Does it hurt a little bit or a whole lot?"

"It's real, real bad, Mama. Can Fannie fix it like she fixed the monster?" Wrapping her slender arms around her self, Becky sniffed back her tears and curled up even more tightly. A low moan escaped her lips.

Anxiety purled down Sarah's spine. This wasn't a usual temperature or ordinary illness, she feared; it was something far more serious.

She soothed her hand across Becky's cheek. "I'll get Fannie."

Hurrying from the room, she went down the hall, a mother's fears for her child's well-being filling her mind. At Fannie's door she rapped once and, without waiting for a response, opened it. Her steps faltered and she swallowed the words she was about to speak.

On the far side of the narrow bed stood a man. He was naked from the waist up, his muscles well developed, his chest had a light scattering of hair, his shoulders broad and skimmed by the length of his blond hair. He was wearing shortened jeans cut raggedly to mid-thigh. Worldly jeans with a zippered fly, not pants with a button flap like those Amish men wore.

He lifted his gaze to meet hers. His familiar light blue eyes held a hint of surprise.

"Who...are you?" she asked, her voice cracking.

Chapter Six

"Don't be afraid, Sarah. I'm not going to hurt you." He took a step toward her, and Sarah retreated outside the bedroom door, back into the shadows of the hallway. Back to where she felt *safe*.

"I need the healer. Where's the healer?" she pleaded, foolishly trying to mentally erase what she had just seen. What she could *still* see.

"I'm no healer, Sarah. I'm Ben. Ben Miller. I've been looking for you for a long time. We lived together in Philadelphia before your accident."

Wings of panic beat in her chest, and she shook her head in denial. "I don't know you. I've *never* known you!" There was no brick building like the one that popped into her mind, no man waiting for her when she came home to a tiny apartment where she grew flowers in a pot on the windowsill. It was an illusion. A dream.

"You were studying to be a nurse but first you had to get your GED. You went to night school at the same time I was getting my contractor's license.

I used to quiz you about muscles and bones and lungs for your biology tests. Stuff like that. You'd ask me questions about electrical codes that I was studying. We laughed because we thought it would be funny if we got the two classes mixed up and took the wrong tests.''

Frantically she looked up and down the hallway in the insane hope of finding an explanation for this man being in her house. An impostor, not a healer. A man who claimed to know her. "I've never needed an education like that. It would make me too worldly.''

"You'd given up everything—your family, your home—to be a nurse so you could save babies' lives. Like your brothers and sisters.''

"No!'' she cried. Pain shot through her temple. She edged down the hallway toward Becky's room. *Her* baby was sick. Sarah didn't have time to listen to this stranger. She couldn't listen. The ache was too great—in her head, in her heart. "Don't say things like that. It's a lie.''

He followed her. Not threatening, really, but all the while doggedly pursuing her. "It's true, Sarah. We lived together for three months. We were lovers, Sarah.''

"I wouldn't—'' She nearly screamed. The accusation hurt. And yet, deep inside, her body clenched in intimate places as though giving credence to his words. "It's not permitted—''

"I loved you, Sarah. And you loved me.'' He spoke softly—with conviction—but it was a lie. It had to be. She'd married Amos. Had lain with him.

Had given birth to his child. There had been no other man. Ever!

She gaped at her accuser, taking in the sharply familiar features of his face—the long, straight nose, the firm, angular jaw, intriguing lips that tempted even as he uttered lies about her. A man's face—as she had suspected all along. How had she been so blind not to see through his disguise from the first?

Perhaps she hadn't wanted to, she thought, shocking herself with that possibility.

But why? She didn't know this stranger. She'd never had a lover. That was forbidden. Unforgivable. *An offense punishable by shunning.* She'd lose everything, *everyone* she knew and loved.

"Mama! It hurts, Mama!"

Becky's cries tore her thoughts from the foul falsehoods the stranger spoke.

"What's wrong with Becky?" Ben asked, his fair eyebrows lowering into a frown.

"I don't know," she answered, whirling toward her daughter's room. Her baby—the most precious thing in the world—needed a healer. Or maybe a doctor. Not a strange man in the house who made Sarah question her sanity, a man who wanted to give form and substance to that empty time in her past that she could not remember; did not *dare* remember.

Please God. She could not have done those things he'd said.

Ben started after her, then realized he couldn't go barging into Becky's room without a shirt on.

He hadn't wanted Sarah to learn who he was this way. He'd meant to let her find out the truth gradually, after she'd learned to trust him. And after she'd remembered at least a little on her own.

No such luck. Instead, her sudden appearance in his room when he was only half dressed had traumatized her.

Hell! Used to be she *liked* seeing him naked— and he liked her that way, too.

Too worried about Becky to take the time to put on his Amish disguise, he grabbed a T-shirt and pulled it on as he headed for Becky's room at a near run.

Sarah was sitting on the bed trying to soothe Becky, who was whimpering and crying. It just about broke Ben's heart to see the little girl in so much pain. What the devil was the matter with her? he wondered.

"Fannie, make it go away," Becky pleaded. Her pretty blue eyes filled with tears and she didn't seem to notice—or care—that he wasn't dressed in his usual clothes. "It hurts."

Kneeling beside the bed, Ben stroked the child's feverish forehead. "I'll try, little Miss Muffet. I'll try...."

Sarah shot him a questioning look. "Do you really know anything about—"

"I know she's got a temperature way the hell over a hundred, and we aren't going to mess around with any herbs. I'm going to get her to the hospital."

"You'll have to call from the phone booth—"

"That car John keeps at the Hosettler's place, is the key in it?"

Her eyes widened. "Under the floor mat, I think. Most boys leave them there but you can't drive. It's not—"

"You just watch me, sweetheart. It's the fastest way to get Becky to the hospital in Peacock and that's what we're gonna do." Standing, he tried to give the child an encouraging smile, all the time his stomach knotting with fear. "You're gonna be okay, pumpkin. I'll go get the car, and your mom will get you ready and downstairs. Five minutes." Slanting a sharp look at Sarah to crush any further objection, he raced downstairs and out of the house.

The work he did kept him in reasonable shape but he wasn't normally a world-class sprinter. Tonight he found a reservoir of speed he'd never before tapped.

HIS ADRENALINE WAS still pumping hard when he pulled the '67 Chevy in front of Sarah's porch. God, what he wouldn't give for his Bronco. The motor of this relic had been cranky, taking three tries before the engine caught. Fear congealed in his gut as Sarah climbed into the back seat, the bundled child in her arms.

En route to the hospital, he didn't sweat the small stuff, like stop signs or even the one signal in town that always seemed to be red. At this hour—now close to midnight—the rural roads were mostly empty, the sidewalks in the village long since deserted.

He slid the car to a stop at the emergency entrance to the hospital and hit the horn long and hard. Before he was even out of the car, a nurse and orderly appeared. The orderly scooped Becky into his arms and carried the child inside. Sarah followed him. As much as Ben wanted to do the same, he figured he'd better go park the car before some overeager security guard decided to have it towed away.

By the time he got back inside, he found Sarah standing alone in one of those typically bleak hospital hallways lined with plastic chairs and unused gurneys. She looked small and vulnerable, her beige dress limp from the day's heat and humidity, her capped head bowed as though her spirit were broken.

He desperately wanted to take her in his arms. To reassure her. To lend whatever strength he had to ease her fears, which had to be a hell of a lot bigger than his own. And his were pretty damn monstrous. He never would have thought he'd care so much about a little kid, a child who wasn't even his own. But he'd connected with Becky in ways he'd hadn't thought possible—probably because she was a lot like her mom.

She looked up as he approached. A double dose of confusion and fear was written in her beautiful blue eyes.

"Where's Becky?" he asked.

"The doctor is with her. They asked me to wait out here. I don't understand why…"

Her voice broke and Ben did just exactly what

he'd vowed not to do. He took Sarah in his arms and held her tight. It felt like heaven to have her right where she belonged, and he inhaled deeply of her familiar herbal scent. When she trembled against him, a throaty groan escaped from his lips.

"They'll take good care of Becky," he whispered, his cheek resting on Sarah's stiff organdy cap. She was a little thinner than she had been six years ago, except for her breasts. They pressed against his chest, full and womanly. If her little girl hadn't been so sick, Ben would have ached with the need to hold Sarah even more intimately. But he was worried, too. There'd be time for that later—he hoped.

To Sarah's dismay, she fit into Fannie's— *Ben's*—embrace as comfortably as if he had always held her. As if all he had said about them being "lovers" were true. She knew that couldn't be. Still, she cherished his strength and calm reassurance. His surprising masculinity. For now, while Becky was so desperately ill, Sarah would lean on this stranger. For her child, she would draw on whatever fortitude he was willing to share. And then later…

No, she couldn't think about that now. Becky was her only concern.

The door behind her swished open, and Sarah turned. The doctor was a huge bearish man with a round face, big belly and squinty, friendly eyes.

"Mrs. Yoder," the doctor said. He glanced at Ben, who looked out of place escorting an Amish when he was wearing cutoffs and a T-shirt.

"Just tell us about Becky," Ben insisted.

"Please, may I see her again?" Sarah pleaded. "She's so afraid—"

"In just a minute." He eyed Ben again, then turned to Sarah. "Looks like an acute case of appendicitis. Her white blood cell count is extremely high, and by palpation her appendix is quite tender. I'd say we were lucky you got here before it burst."

Placing her hand on her chest, Sarah took a deep, painful breath. Her heart was pounding so hard she was sure the doctor could hear it. "You'll do surgery, then?" she asked.

"It's the best course, and we should do it immediately." His forehead puckered with a frown. "Our only problem at the moment is that Becky has type-O blood and we're fresh out of reserves."

"How can you be out of type-O, Doc?" Ben asked, obviously irritated. "That's universal. Any hospital worth its salt—"

Sarah placed a restraining hand on his arm.

"Unfortunately there was a major accident on the highway earlier this evening, a car and a buggy colliding. One fatality and several injured."

"Oh, I'm so sorry…" Sarah instinctively murmured, although her primary worry was for her daughter.

"Normally in Amish country our big call is for type-A blood and O we use for a backup reserve," the doctor explained. "It seems that most everyone hereabouts is the one type. Runs in the families, you see."

"Then how is it my Becky is an O?" Sarah recalled from Amos's last hospitalization that his blood type had been A. She thought hers was the same, though at the moment she was so upset about Becky she couldn't remember for sure.

The doctor shrugged his massive shoulders. "Usually there's not a problem about needing a transfusion with an appendectomy anyway. I only mention the problem so you'll be informed."

Ben asked, "Are you saying it'd be safer if you had some type-O blood on hand?"

"I like to be prepared for any eventuality, even a remote one."

"Then take my blood, Doc. I'm O-positive."

In relief, Sarah turned to Ben, grateful that he was here and willing to donate his blood. No matter what the doctor said, Becky's life could depend on that.

"Are you sure?" the doctor asked.

"Yeah, I give blood a couple of times a year. It's no big deal."

"And it's been a while since you've given?"

"Four or five months, I'd say."

"Fine, then. If it's all right with Mrs. Yoder, we'll set you up to donate blood, and I'll have them prepare the O.R. for Becky."

"Yes, please, Doctor. Do whatever is necessary." She wanted her little girl back safe and healthy, and was willing to pay any price, even if it meant this disturbing stranger's blood would flow through Becky's veins.

HURRYING, BEN TOOK THE stairs to the second floor two at a time to the blood center. He was scared for Becky and wanted to be with Sarah. He knew how worried she was, and she'd need someone with her after they took Becky in for the operation.

Something else niggled at the back of his brain, too—something not quite right, but he couldn't put his finger on it because anxiety about Becky and Sarah consumed him. An idea, a thought, kept flitting around like a hyperactive mosquito.

A night nurse settled him into one of the lounging chairs and he held out his arm so she could get a good shot at his vein.

"Just relax" the nurse said.

"Let's get on with it." Leaning back, he gazed up at the acoustic ceiling and fluorescent lights. He sighed, forcing his taut muscles to relax. Becky would be fine. So would Sarah. She was a strong woman with a solid core of steel, as tough and determined when she needed to be as any man who walked the girders in a high-rise. Yet wrapped around all that steel was a gentleness, a sweetness that drew Ben like a nail to a magnet.

He remembered he'd been the one to release her hidden passions. She'd taken to lovemaking with the fervor of a woman who'd just discovered her own sexuality—and enjoyed every moment of exploration.

That first time—their first time together—had shaken everything Ben had thought he'd known about women. If he hadn't loved Sarah before that night, she had certainly claimed his heart then. And forever. Yes, he remembered every detail of that night....

"HEY, BEN, YOU CAME in late this morning and now you're checking out right on the button." The construction foreman on the job in Philadelphia tipped his hard hat back and grinned at Ben. "Wouldn't have somethin' to do with that pretty little lady I saw you with last week, would it?"

"None of your business, Mac." Ben strapped his lunch pail on the back of his Harley and mounted. Damn right, his hurry to get home had to do with Sarah. The kisses they'd shared that morning had only whetted his appetite for more—a *whole* lot more.

Would she feel the same way?

He stopped at a grocery store to pick up the fixings for spaghetti and a salad. After a day's work as a hospital aide, Sarah had a class till six, and Ben wanted dinner ready when she got home. He wanted everything to be perfect. And he didn't want any long delays, not with the plans—and hopes— he had for the evening.

After showering, he put the water on to boil, dumped the package of lettuce into a bowl, and set the table, sticking the festive red candles he'd bought in a couple of juice glasses. He noticed his hands were shaking. If he'd been the first man to kiss Sarah, he'd be her first lover, too.

But only if she was ready for the next step.

He'd be gentle with her, he swore he would. No way did he want to hurt her.

He'd known his fair share of women over the years. Until now, his relationships had been pretty casual. This one, with Sarah, was for keeps.

If she'd have him.

The door opened, and Ben caught his breath. Even dressed in the unflattering pink pantsuit uniform, even after a busy shift at the hospital making beds and handling bedpans, she was beautiful. Her lustrous eyes reflected serenity and goodness— daunting qualities for a guy like Ben who'd always believed he was practically the spawn of the devil—until Sarah had come along, that is, and he'd begun to think he was worthy of being loved by someone like her.

"What's this?" she asked, tilting her head as she took in the small table set for two, the candles, the paper napkins he'd folded into a pyramid at each place. She laid her schoolbooks on the desk by the window.

"I figured you'd be tired. Long day with your class and all." Self-conscious, he stuffed his hands in his jeans pockets. Maybe this had been a really dumb idea. Maybe she wouldn't want to—

"You've been cooking dinner?"

"Spaghetti. All that's left to do is put the noodles in the water. Whenever you're ready."

Smiling her gentle smile—the one that made Ben's chest tighten almost painfully with emotion—she crossed the cramped living room and wrapped her arms around his waist. "I didn't know how lucky I was the night you rescued me—Benjamin Miller, my knight in shining armor. I couldn't have found a better man.''

He reciprocated by drawing her closer, her lips temptingly near. "I've never met anyone like you, Sarah. You're like a dream come true. I don't deserve you. But that doesn't stop me from wanting you.''

His senses had never been so alert. Beneath his palm, the slick polyester fabric of her slacks molded to the curve of her hips. Inhaling, he caught the sweet fragrance of her shampoo and her subtler essence that was herbal, the combination intoxicating. She wore her hair coiled at her nape, as she had while living as a member of the Amish community. But sometimes, on her days off, she let it hang long and loose. Ben's fingers itched to loosen her hair now, to bunch those flaxen, silken strands in his hands.

"I have been very wicked today," she confessed.

He raised his brows.

"All day long I have thought of nothing but the way you kissed me this morning. Miss Caldecott had to remind me twice to pick up the trays on the fifth floor. I was that distracted.''

He grinned. "Me, too. I nearly walked right off the end of a girder without looking.''

"Oh, my." Her eyes sparkled with impish amusement. "Whatever are we to do?''

Brushing a kiss against her forehead, he said, "I know what I want to do. I even—well, I didn't have any—you know, protection. So at the store… But I don't want to rush you, Sarah. You set the pace.''

Meanwhile, he'd probably die a thousand painful deaths if she made him wait too long.

"Protection?"

He flushed. "Condoms. Just in case..."

"You bought condoms so I wouldn't get pregnant?" Her forehead puckered into a tiny frown. Rising up on her toes, she placed a fleeting kiss on his lips. "Someday, Benjamin Andrew Miller, I would like very much to have your babies."

Ben's knees went weak with the sheer joy of her promise, and he groaned. "Oh, yeah, Sweet Sarah. I'll give you as many babies as you want. We'll save up and buy a house, and get married. Then we'll fill that house with all the babies you can handle." And Ben would have the family he'd dreamed about; a family he'd only thought existed on a TV screen.

He lowered his head, his mouth claiming hers. Later he'd been sure his promise of marriage had been what allowed Sarah to ease her strict moral conviction. That and her love for him.

"That's it, Mr. Miller."

His eyes flew open as the nurse removed the needle from his arm. Momentarily disoriented, he blinked against the bright overhead lights.

She wrapped a stretch bandage around his arm and bent his elbow to keep the pressure on. "You rest for a minute and I'll get you some orange juice."

"I'm fine." He sat up, taking just enough time to make sure he wasn't going to get dizzy. He didn't want to hang around here when Sarah needed him. *And Becky,* her daughter, needed him too.

He frowned. In the heat of those first weeks of discovering each other, he hadn't been a hundred-percent careful about using a condom. Most times, sure. But once when he'd caught her in the shower, he'd forgotten about using protection. Hell, he'd forgotten about everything except being inside her slick, warm heat.

And there'd been that lazy Sunday morning they'd spent in bed, the snow falling outside. She'd been in a teasing mood. Strategically applied straw-berry jelly had shot every rational thought from his mind.

Maybe there'd been other times, too. He didn't remember. And condoms were never a hundred-percent sure.

God! Could it be? His chest filled with the pos-sibility. Did he dare jump to that conclusion without checking the facts? How could he not?

He took the stairs to the first floor, the hospital eerily silent in the early hours of the new day, and found the surgical waiting room.

Sarah looked up as he came in. A dizzying sense of relief washed over her. She didn't have to face the ordeal of waiting alone. Almost instantly, she tried to press the thought aside. This stranger, with his wild stories and accusations, should be of no comfort to her at all. Instead she should be sending him to bring Samuel here—the man she would marry, the man who would soon be Becky's father.

She drew a shaky breath and clasped her hands

in her lap, her courage to send the stranger away deserting her.

"They've already taken Becky into the O.R.?" Ben asked.

She nodded.

He slid into the chair next to her, his shorts and hairy legs shocking when she had so recently thought he was a woman. She forced herself to glance away.

"How long will it be?" he asked.

"A couple of hours. Perhaps more."

"You should try to get some sleep."

Her head lifted and his light blue eyes snared her. Eyes, she realized, that were almost the same shade as Becky's. Her throat tightened in fear and confusion. "I couldn't sleep a wink."

He glanced at his wrist, as though he might be used to wearing a watch, and she detected a band of skin less tanned than the rest. Why hadn't she noticed that before? Why hadn't she suspected that nothing about her house guest was as it had seemed to be?

"Then let's go find some coffee." Standing, he extended his hand.

She stared at his blunt fingers, a palm callused by hard work. Not the hand of a woman, but instead that of a lover? Did she even want to know?

"Come on," he urged. "We can talk while we're waiting."

As though she'd become a robot and Benjamin Miller held the controls, she slipped her hand into his. The fit was like pulling on an old, familiar glove, warm and comforting against the cold. She shivered; her temple throbbed. What terrible things had she done in the past she couldn't remember?

The second-floor coffee shop was empty, the lights dimmed. He chose a table near the windows. In the parking lot, scattered cars reflected the glow of streetlights like lonely sentinels. From somewhere Ben returned with two cups of coffee. Hers had the extra cream she liked. Had he noticed that since he'd been living in her home? Or had he known that before as he'd claimed?

He pulled out the chair next to her, turned it around, straddling it in a thoroughly masculine way. "Okay, why don't we start with what you *do* remember?"

"If you're going to tell me more lies, I have no interest in listening. My child—"

"Do you remember wanting to be a nurse?"

She turned away. "I was just a child then, with childish thoughts." And rebellious and sure that she knew better than her parents, she remembered with a wash of shame. "An Amish woman doesn't need—"

"But you remember."

"Oh, all right!" Her nerves teetered near the breaking point. "My brothers and sisters had died needlessly, because they hadn't had vaccinations. And then one day at the drug store I saw a magazine. There was an article inside that said people like Short Martha, if they were given growth hormones when they were young, they'd grow taller. I thought—"

"I didn't know that," he said in surprise. "You never mentioned Martha."

"She has always been my friend." Head bent, she clasped the paper cup, the coffee nearly burning her palms. "Helping her was a foolish dream."

"A dream you tried to make come true."

"No," she said softly. "I wouldn't have done that. As much as I love Martha and know her heart aches because no man has chosen her for a wife, I would *not* have left my home. Besides, there would have been no way for me to help her then. It was too late. We were both nearly grown."

"But it wouldn't have been too late for others like her who might come along. And for other babies who needed immunizations."

"Please, you don't know what you're talking about."

He speared his fingers through his hair, a darker blond than her own and variegated by the sun. Lines of tension and fatigue tightened around his eyes and rimmed his full lips. Yet, beneath it all, he was a ruggedly handsome man. Why hadn't she realized...?

"Do you remember those gangbangers who tried to rough you up near the bus depot?"

She gasped. How could Benjamin Miller know of the recurring nightmare that crept into her dreams? "Of course not," she burst out. "No such thing has ever happened to me."

With lifted brows, he questioned her statement. "How 'bout the guy on the motorcycle who rescued you?"

"I don't know what you're talking about." The sound of an engine being revved roared in her head. A car leaving the hospital parking lot, she told herself, or possibly a motorcycle. *Not a memory.* To keep her own sanity, she didn't dare believe her dreams—or Benjamin Miller.

Shoving himself up from the table, he paced around the room. "You loved to grow flowers even in the dead of winter and the flowered scarf I bought you was the first patterned thing you'd ever worn. You were so proud of it and covered your head with that scarf every time you went out. You said watching TV was too worldly, but you were fascinated by all the shows, even when I made you watch football, which you thought was too violent. You liked to listen to my Tina Turner and Rod Stewart tapes. And sometimes we danced in the living room."

"Stop it!" she hissed.

"One time we rode the train to D.C. and we saw the Capitol and all the museums. We stayed at a hotel and ordered room service. You laughed and said it was the most decadent, wonderful thing you'd ever done."

"Please!" She leaped to her feet. Tears clogged her throat and burned her eyes. "I don't remember any of that. I don't *want* to remember."

"Well, I *can't* forget, Sarah. You've got a tiny strawberry mark right there." He touched her—intimately—his fingertips caressing her left breast.

Her flesh burned as though he had branded her,

and desire bloomed—incredibly—low in her body. "How could you know…" she sobbed.

"I loved you too much to forget *anything* about you. And this is what I remember the best."

Before she knew what was happening, he'd taken her in his arms, his mouth claiming hers in a fierce kiss. She couldn't breathe; she couldn't think. She could only feel. Tormenting sensations of heat and desire sped through her, challenging her sanity. Reckless feelings so staggering she went weak all over, unable to resist the caress of his tongue, the way he crossed and recrossed her lips with his. Probing deeper. Always deeper.

With exquisite familiarity.

She was aware of every detail of him. The taste of coffee on his tongue. His muscular physique. The breadth of his shoulders. His powerful arms around her. Through the fabric of his jeans, she felt the press of his potent arousal against her midsection.

A purring sound hummed in her throat, aching there where she felt so full of emotion and need. Except the most insistent need was making itself known much lower in her body. Embarrassingly so. And it throbbed like a drum—pulsing in a primitive rhythm—a rhythm her body knew and remembered, even if her mind resisted the possibility.

Twisting her face away, she shoved at his unyielding chest. "Stop," she ordered, her voice hoarse and breathless.

His hold on her eased—barely. "You're going to remember, Sarah. There's no way you could forget what we had together. I won't *let* you."

Chapter Seven

"You'll come back, won't you?"

Becky's blue eyes looked sleepy with the residual effects of anesthesia, her eyelids drooping. Tiny and vulnerable in the hospital bed, she snuggled with the huge panda bear Ben had purchased in the gift shop. Hell, if Sarah had let him, Ben would have bought out the entire stock of teddy bears.

He understood why Sarah was reluctant to leave her child after the surgery, even to get some much-needed rest of her own. But she was dead on her feet. For that matter, Ben was running on his reserves, too.

"We'll be back, Miss Muffet, I promise," he said.

Sarah, her features drawn taut with fatigue, caressed her daughter's cheek one more time. "You need your rest. I have to feed the chickens and take care of our horse. You take a nap and I'll be back by suppertime."

"Do I gots to stay here all night?"

"The doctor says you must. But tomorrow you'll

be home again.'' She bent down over the bed's guardrail to kiss Becky's forehead. ''I am glad you're such a strong, brave little girl. Sleep safe.''

''Bye, Fannie.'' She waggled her fingers at him. ''Thank you for the panda.''

''You're welcome...munchkin.'' His voice cracked.

''Don't foget to put on your dress like proper Amish women are s'posed to wear,'' Becky reminded him.

''I'll remember.'' Emotion crowded in his chest. The impossible had happened. He was pretty damn sure of it. He felt like shouting the news from the top of the highest building in town. ''I'll see you at dinner.''

On the drive home, Sarah leaned back and closed her eyes. Ben didn't think she was asleep. More likely she was avoiding conversation. He'd laid a lot on her about their past together. He'd have to give her a little time to absorb what he'd told her. Then he'd break the rest of the news to her.

He grimaced and rubbed his hand across his whiskered cheeks. Now that he'd found Sarah—and Becky—patience was not going to be his long suit. If it ever had been.

Sarah got out of the car as soon as he pulled to a stop in front of the house. Switching off the ignition, he hurried to follow her onto the porch.

''I want you out of my house as soon as possible,'' she said, turning to block his way.

''I don't think so, Sarah. We still have some unfinished business.''

"You and I have never had business together. And never will."

"That's where you're dead wrong."

She glanced around as if she were afraid someone would see them talking on the porch. "Even if what you say is true—which I will deny with my last breath—you have no right to be here now. No right to meddle in my life. You came into my home under false pretenses, lying to me, to my daughter and to all of my friends." Angry spots of red colored her cheeks. "Now I want you gone."

He leaned one hand on the doorjamb beside her, effectively barring her retreat. "What month was Becky born?"

She blinked at his quick change of subject. "July. She just turned five last month. But that has nothing to do with—"

"We were together from before Halloween till right after New Year's. Six years ago."

"I've told you, I don't believe—"

Ben watched her eyes widen as the impact of what he'd said sank in. Myriad emotions crossed her face like a series of violent summer storms— shock, horror, fear and finally a return to denial.

"No!" she said, snapping the word out as if Ben would go away if she denied the truth firmly enough.

"The doctor said most of the Amish families around here have type-A blood. What kind of blood did Amos have?"

Her face paled. "It doesn't matter now. He's

dead." Turning, she tried to tug open the screen door. Ben held it firmly closed.

"What's your blood type, Sarah?"

"I don't know! Go away!" Her back to him, she shook her head so hard her cap wobbled. "I don't want you here."

"Sarah. Sweetheart," he cajoled. He leaned close, brushing his lips against the side of her neck. "I think we made a baby together. A beautiful little girl. I think I'm Becky's father."

His announcement hung suspended in the air like an executioner's ax poised above his victim's neck. Ben could hardly breathe waiting for her reaction. The entire county seemed to be holding its breath. No buggies clopped down the road; the birds and bees had suddenly fallen silent. She couldn't send him away now—not when she knew Becky was his daughter, too.

She turned, her eyes filled with tears. "That's not possible. I lay only with Amos. I was *his* wife."

"Count the months, Sarah. She's mine."

"Becky was a little premature. It doesn't mean—"

"She and I have the same type of blood. Explain that—"

"That doesn't prove anything." Catching him off guard, she yanked open the screen and unlatched the door.

He shoved in through the door before she could shut it in his face. "DNA tests would prove my paternity."

"You can't do this! I won't let you take my baby

away from me! I won't!'' Nearly hysterical, she ran toward the kitchen.

Ben caught up with her just as she was pulling a carving knife from the drawer. ''For God's sake, Sarah.'' He grabbed her wrist. ''I don't want to take Becky away from you. I want us to be a family— you and me and our baby. All the babies you ever wanted.'' Wild-eyed, she tried to wrench her hand free.

''Jenny's Michael came with the sheriff,'' she sobbed. ''He took her babies. All three of them. I couldn't live without—'' She flailed at him with her free hand, clipping his chin with her fist.

Ben didn't know what was going on. He didn't know who Michael was or why Sarah was so hysterical. He only knew he had to calm her down, so he twisted the knife from her hand and pulled her into his arms. He held her tight. She tried to punch him, and kicked him in the shin. He didn't let go. Finally she collapsed against him, crying so hard her body shook.

Staring over the top of her head, he was scared spitless he was going to lose Sarah again, and Becky, too, and he'd only just found them both. The woman he loved and *his* little girl. Raised as another man's child.

''I'm not going to take Becky away from you,'' he whispered again when Sarah's sobbing had quieted to a few little sniffles.

''Jenny's husband is taking her babies.'' She sniffed and her body shuddered one more time.

Relaxing his hold, he dug in his pants pocket for

a handkerchief. "All I want is a chance to get to know her—for us to know each other. I want to stay here with you."

She lifted her face, her eyes red-rimmed from crying, and blew her nose. "I can't have a man staying in my house. I'm a widow. Our customs don't allow—"

"I'll keep masquerading as a woman—Fannie, the healer. No one has figured it out." Except Short Martha, he suspected, and he didn't think she'd blow his cover though he wasn't quite sure why she hadn't already. "Yesterday, at the barn raising, they all thought I walked on water 'cause I helped that kid."

"I don't know...." She hesitated, but maybe it was only because she was afraid he'd snatch Becky away from her.

"Look, we can all go on picnics together, like the two of us did in Philadelphia. Maybe we can go fishing. You told me you liked fishing."

She nodded cautiously as though reluctant to admit he knew anything about her personal likes and dislikes.

"The more time we spend together, the more likely you are to get your memory back. And you'll remember me."

"I don't want to—"

"You're scared because deep inside you know I'm telling you the truth about us."

"You mustn't tell Becky who you are. That you think you're her father. It will be bad enough when she starts asking other questions about you. She's Amos's child, not yours."

Her insistence on that lie slammed into Ben's gut like a crowbar hitting his midsection. "I won't tell her who I am. For now."

Her chin trembled, and he thought she was going to start crying again. "In less than a month's time I'm to marry Samuel."

"Then give me that much time, Sarah," he pleaded, desperate. He'd give every dime he had if only she'd remember their past; but all the money in the world couldn't buy him her love. "If you don't remember me by then...if you don't want me—I won't bother you anymore. I'll go away." Dear God, it cost him a lot to make that promise. It was a price he didn't want to pay.

"You'll leave Becky alone? You won't take her with you?"

He swallowed hard. How could he promise a thing like that? He wanted to be Becky's dad almost as much as he wanted Sarah to be his wife—for them all to be a family. He knew he could hire a high-price attorney, go to court, and probably get joint custody. But this was one time when his money wasn't going to do him any good. If he threatened to take Sarah's child away she'd hate him. Yet he sensed that that very possibility would allow him one last chance to make Sarah love him again. She was afraid to lose Becky like this Jenny person had apparently lost her children.

He screwed up his courage, ready to risk everything on one last draw of the cards.

"For now, we'll play by your rules, Sarah, as long as you let me stay. But I *am* Becky's father. I know it as sure as I'm standing here. And I have rights, too."

Fear forced Sarah to give a reluctant nod of agreement. What choice did she have? This stranger might say he wouldn't take her daughter away, but she wasn't sure she could trust him.

She wasn't sure she could trust herself.

"I must feed the chickens," she said, slipping away from Ben and hurrying out the back door. Even if she went to her room, she wouldn't be able to sleep. Her emotions were too volatile.

How did Benjamin Miller know such intimate details about her? She doubted Amos had ever noted the slight birth mark on her breast, and he certainly had never remarked on it, yet this stranger had touched her there. Unerringly. As though he'd seen her naked. More than once.

Her heart throbbed in her throat as she scooped feed into a pail in the shed, then stepped into the chicken coop. The rooster strutted over demanding to know why she was late, his harem of hens squawking and fluttering in his wake. She tossed out a handful of grain and the chickens scattered to peck up the kernels.

Could what Ben Miller have said possibly be true?

Concentrating, she tried to unearth images of that day she'd awakened in the hospital. It had been so long ago. No one, not her parents or her husband, had ever spoken again of that time.

"Where am I, Mama?" she had asked. "What happened to me, Papa?" Her parents were standing beside her bed. Her father's long beard did nothing to hide his dour, disapproving expression. In contrast, her mother appeared on the verge of tears.

"You were warned and still you disobeyed me," her father said, his tone disapproving.

What had she done wrong? Sarah wondered frantically, her hand lifting unsteadily to touch the wide bandage that swathed her head. Her stomach felt uneasy, her body ached. In the face of her father's condemnation, guilt for unknown sins washed over her. Desperately she wanted her father to look on her with favor—to love her again.

She shot a plea for understanding toward her mother, who simply shook her head.

"We'll be taking you home now," her father said.

"Let her rest a bit, husband," Sarah's mother pleaded. "She's only just now awake, *ja?*"

"What's wrong with me?" Sarah asked. "What have I done?"

Her mother looked as if she wanted to say something, but her father spoke first. "You will marry Amos Yoder come Sunday next."

"Marry?" Sarah's eyes widened. She barely knew the man. He lived in a neighboring community…and he was near the age of her parents, not one of the boys who might have courted her—

"You will not be breaking your promises again."

"But, Papa, I don't remember—"

"Get her ready to leave this place," her father

ordered, terminating the conversation. Abruptly, he whirled and marched out of the room, leaving Sarah's mother to help her get dressed.

Though Sarah had pleaded for an explanation, none had been forthcoming from her mother. And when she'd returned home, everyone seemed to know she had promised to marry Amos. Strangely, only Sarah had forgotten her vow. The community expected her to keep her promise.

When had she agreed to marry Amos Yoder? As a widower he would not have taken her to the Sunday-night singings young couples enjoyed as part of their courtship. Though she recalled seeing him at barn raisings and funerals, her memory failed her when it came to having more than a few casual words with the man. When had they come to care for each other? And if she had once loved him, why had her feelings during their marriage been only those of respect and duty?

What had she done so terribly wrong that her father would force a marriage on her that she had not sought? That had *never* been the way of the Amish community.

She reached into the pail of chicken feed only to find it empty. While lost in the past, she had scattered every grain of it.

Dear heaven! Could her parents have known she was *pregnant* with the stranger's child?

The possibilities if that were true—the depth of their betrayal—staggered her.

No, she mentally back-tracked, her parents were good people, her father a church elder. Though stern and steeped in the traditions of their faith, they had never lied to her. It was unthinkable.

But the tortuous questions remained. Had they known of Benjamin Miller? And had they kept an even more desperate secret from her?

Did she dare confront them with her suspicions?

IN SPITE OF HERSELF, Sarah smiled at the sight of Ben in his organdy cap and women's garb teaching Becky to thread a worm onto a hook. Becky had been home from the hospital a week now, and the doctor had said she was well enough for a buggy ride.

Sarah marveled at the fact she had not known from the beginning that Ben was a man. In these past few days, despite her fears and confusion, she'd seen him in a new light, particularly since during the evenings, after Becky had gone to bed and no one was likely to drop by, he now wore his jeans. He was thoroughly male in every way—now that she knew his secret—he'd been kind and gentle with Becky, and patient with Sarah without pressing her for more than she was willing to give.

Which, at this point, was very little. He represented danger. The loss of all she held dear. She wished he'd never come here; she wished he were gone.

But he persisted.

In recent years she had felt content with her life. True, in the early days of her marriage she had chafed at Amos's humorless ways—much the way she had bristled under her father's strict discipline. But she had adjusted. And after Becky's arrival, her life had taken on new meaning and a deeper happiness. She'd gained a sense of purpose she'd formerly been lacking.

Where restrictions had bothered her before, those same limitations represented stability after she'd become a mother. Rules she'd hated as a child made sense from a parent's point of view. Over time she'd learned to appreciate her Amish lifestyle more than she had thought possible and felt her daughter would be safe raised among the plain people of the settlement.

Now Ben had upset the delicate balance she'd achieved. Suddenly her life was as tangled as uncombed hair in the morning.

With a troubled sigh, she spread a picnic blanket on the ground beneath a cottonwood tree. She had chosen a spot where the creek meandered through rolling farmland, dipping occasionally into a deep fishing hole, and cottonwoods lined the banks providing shade to ease the summer heat. No sound of civilization intruded upon the secluded hollow. The buggy horse munched contentedly on the long grass where he was hobbled. A hawk drifted in lazy circles across a nearly cloudless sky, and a single butterfly flitted among the last wildflower blooms of the season.

Were Sarah's thoughts not in such turmoil, she would have been content in this peaceful setting.

"Okay, here we go." Standing, Ben grasped the pole with Becky and they tossed the line into the water. The orange bobber landed with a quiet sploosh.

"Now what do we do?" Becky asked.

"Now we wait."

The child scowled. "How long?"

"Till some big ole fish comes along and gobbles up our worm. You've gotta watch that bobber real close so he doesn't steal our bait without us catching him."

Her forehead pleating in the same way that Ben's sometimes did, Becky said, "I hope he comes quick."

The encouraging squeeze Ben gave the child's shoulder constricted Sarah's heart. In spite of her inability to remember the past, it was possible that he was Becky's father.

Leaving Becky sitting on the grassy bank, fishing pole in hand, Ben sprawled out on the picnic quilt next to Sarah. Lying on his side, he propped his head in his hand. "Pretty terrific day, huh?"

"*Ja,*" she agreed. "Did we…" She hesitated. If she asked too many questions, she might be forced to face an unpleasant truth about herself.

Or she might learn that Ben had concocted the whole story and it was nothing but lies.

"What?"

"You said we went on picnics together."

"Yeah." The suggestion of a dimple creased his cheek, and a surprising flutter coursed through Sarah's midsection. "Froze our buns off, too. It was November. There hadn't been any snow yet but it was pretty darn cold. We bundled up like we were going to the North Pole.''

''I made fried chicken?'' That's what she'd brought today, along with potato salad, zucchini bread and fresh peaches.

''Nope. We had hoagies, chips and pop. It was your birthday, November 23rd, and I couldn't afford to take you out to a fancy dinner, so you said you wanted to go on a picnic.'' He plucked a blade of grass and tucked the stem between his teeth. ''I figured it wasn't right you had to make the fixings, too.''

Sarah felt herself pale and self-consciously straightened her long skirt over her legs. *He knew her birthday.* What other private details of her life might he know? *Besides* the mark on her breast.

''What kind of work do you do?'' she asked, wanting to direct the topic away from her...and more curious about Ben than she was willing to admit.

''I'm in construction. Mostly commercial high-rises. Some residential projects.''

A man who worked with his hands. An honorable profession. Somehow she'd known that. Only a man confident of himself and his masculinity could spend his days wearing a dress. ''Do you like what you do?''

''Sure, I guess so. I make a good living now.''

Like most Amish men, Ben, too, would be a good provider. That would be important to him. ''You can be away from your work for so long a time?''

"I've got people who will cover for me."

"I'm sorry if I sound like I'm prying. It's just that I don't remember any of those things that you've told me." Or perhaps it was that she wouldn't take the risk of recalling that other time, that other place, that sometimes haunted her dreams. She rubbed at her temple as fuzzy images of her strolling along a city street hand in hand with a man came to her. But as hard as she tried, she couldn't see his face, nor did she recall being in such a place.

"It's okay." Lying back, Ben stacked his hands behind his head, looking up through the motionless leaves of the cottonwood. "Whatever you want to know, just ask."

She studied him, her gaze sweeping down the length of his physique. Her lips twitched and she swallowed hard. "Ben?"

"Hmm?"

"Your, ah, breasts..."

He cut her a look out of the corner of his eye. "What?"

Flushing, she smothered a laugh with her hand. "They're, ah... Oh, dear. They're all cockeyed."

"Hell, I don't know how you women wear these darn bra things." Sitting, he scooted his bra around, straightening the objects in question to the front of his dress instead to the side.

In spite of her best efforts to keep still, a giggle escaped her. "Perhaps we're built a little differently than you are."

His brows lowering into a scowl, he eyed her. "Sweet Sarah, are you teasing me?"

She shook her head, another giggle erupting.

With a mock snarl, he dived for her, rolling her onto her back, tipping the picnic basket over in the process. His big, masculine body pressed against her, hard where she was soft, trapping her. Awareness flooded through her. Of need. Of wanting. Of feelings she didn't dare either remember—or experience in the here and now. She caught the musky base note of his skin. His fingers tightened ever so slightly around her shoulders, restrained, speaking eloquently of his need for her. Her blood pounded through her veins.

"Ben, *nein*," she whispered. "Please don't."

The moment hung suspended on threads as fine as a spider web. He'd snared her. In his eyes, she saw he'd recognized her momentary weakness. Would he let her go? Or exploit his advantage?

She trembled, waiting, her gaze focused on his sensual lips, unable to decide what she should hope for. Her chest heaved as she drew in a shaky breath. Though she had forgotten the past, she did recall his kiss of a week ago. The press of his lips on hers, the coffee taste of him. How her legs had gone weak. How heat had spiraled through her. Feelings no woman who was planning to marry another man should experience.

"Fannie! Fannie! I catched one!"

Ben held his position for a long moment, his heart thudding hard and heavy in his chest. He wanted to kiss Sarah so much, he ached with the need. But it was not to be. Not with his daughter calling him.

With a sigh, he levered himself away. "I'm going to have to talk to Miss Muffet about her timing."

"No, don't say anything." Panic flashed in Sarah's eyes. "Please."

He caressed her cheek with his fingertips. "I promised, didn't I? Trust me, Sarah."

"Fannie!" Becky wailed. "Help me."

The way Becky was shouting, a man might think she'd landed a whale. Instead, a six-inch shiner dangled from the end of the line.

"He's only a baby, Fannie. Please, please, let him go." A shower of tears erupted and raced down Becky's pudgy little-girl cheeks.

Grinning, Ben grabbed the line. "You mean after going to all this trouble to catch a fish, we're going to let him go?"

"The hook's hurting his mouth, Fannie. I didn't mean to hurt him."

"What about our dinner? I thought we were going to cook up—"

"*Nein, nein! Bitte,* Fannie. Please let him go."

The poor kid was a mess, bubbling hysterically as Ben worked to free the fish. Becky had her mother's compassionate heart, even if only a fish was involved. "Hang on, honey. I'm getting it."

Finally unhooking the fish, Ben scrambled down the bank and eased it into the water. It rolled over onto its side, floating there like a dead fish.

"Come on, fish," he muttered. "The kid's dying

of guilt up there. Do your stuff.'' He gave it a little shove.

The tail twitched; the fish righted itself. A couple more twitches and away it went, heading for the deepest part of the creek.

Ben sat back on his haunches, chuckling softly to himself, then glanced up at Becky on the bank.

''Did I murder him?'' Becky asked forlornly. Her fishing pole forgotten on the ground, she swiped at her face with her arm, smearing her tears on her sleeve.

''Nope. He's already back home with his mom and dad, probably telling them all about his big adventure.''

Ben scrambled up the bank and lifted Becky in his arms. Like her mother, she wore her organdy cap and calf-length dress everywhere she went, and if given a choice, preferred to go barefoot.

''I don't want to catch no more fish today,'' she said, sniffing.

''That's okay, Miss Muffet. How 'bout we eat some of your mom's fried chicken instead?''

When he deposited Becky on the ground, she fled to her mother's side, snuggling close to Sarah for reassurance. A lump the size of the Liberty Bell formed in Ben's throat. A family. That's what the three of them were and that's what he wanted them to be.

But would Sarah be willing to give up everything she'd known, the life she'd led except for their three short months together, to make Ben's dream come true?

Did he even deserve that kind of sacrifice?

Chapter Eight

Sarah laid out a feast on the yellow-and-blue quilt. Ben helped himself to a chicken leg, and she scooped potato salad onto his plate, giving him a couple of carrot sticks for good measure. Then she served Becky.

"I'm not hungry," Becky complained, still puffy-eyed from her cry.

"Eat a little, then you can take a nap here on the blanket."

"But Mama—"

Sarah halted Becky's protest with a censoring lift of her brows. Ben swallowed a smile. Sarah might be softhearted, but she kept a tight rein on her daughter without resorting to shouting or violence.

Ben could hardly ever remember his folks using a civil tone with him. More often than not, discipline at his house had been harsh, a belt applied to his backside where his father said it would do the most good. Ben didn't want to raise his kids that way.

It wasn't long before Becky lay down on her

own, her head in Sarah's lap, and drifted off to sleep. Sarah stroked her daughter's cheek, smoothing back strands of blond hair that had come loose from her cap. Her hair, Sarah realized, was a shade darker than her own and very much the same color as Ben's. In contrast, Amos and all of his sons had nearly black hair.

She pursed her lips. On a mental checklist, she marked one more reason to believe Ben was telling the truth, then quickly slammed the door shut on that train of thought. To admit the possibility that Ben was her child's biological father was to acknowledge that she had grievously sinned. That for the past six years she had been living a lie.

"She looks real comfortable," Ben said, indicating the child resting her head on Sarah's lap. "You got room for one more?"

A flush stole up Sarah's neck and heated her cheeks. "I don't think so." Pillowing Ben's head so intimately would have all kinds of repercussions, most of them related to her desire to touch him, to see if through her tactile sense she could recall what her mind refused to accept.

With a shrug, he shed his cap, laying it aside, and loosened his ponytail. His hair fell free to his shoulders. *Like Samson's,* she thought. Her fingers itched to investigate the texture of the long, blond strands. Would they feel like Becky's hair, or thicker and somehow more masculine?

Like forbidden fruit, everything about Ben intrigued her. She wanted to know how he'd gotten a slight bump on his nose. Had he broken it in a fight, or perhaps while playing sports?

On Fannie, the healer, his strong jaw had seemed out of place. Overpowering. Now the firm lines added to his obvious masculinity.

In spite of the afternoon heat, she shivered as she recalled the feel of his full lips on hers. Tempting her. Demanding a response she couldn't refuse. Even dressed as a woman, Ben was more manly than any of the men she had known—including her late husband.

"I don't know how you women wear those darn bonnets all the time," Ben said. "Aren't they hot?"

"No different than a man wearing a hat." Though at the moment she was sweating, she didn't believe it had anything to do with her cap, or even the weather. The warmth was flooding her from the inside out.

"Hmm, hadn't thought of it like that. But it sure doesn't feel the same as a hard hat." Using a paring knife, he halved a fresh peach, offering her a portion.

"*Nein, danke.*" Although she had refused his offer, she watched, fascinated, as he brought the peach to his mouth. At his first bite, she could almost taste the sweet juice flowing in her own mouth. She swallowed and licked her lips. If he kissed her now, she'd be able to taste the fruit.

Trying to distract herself, she asked, "How is it you wear your hair long?"

"My way of rebelling, I suppose," he said as he took another bite. "Sometimes I have to deal with suits—you know, high-powered businessmen. It's my way of letting them know that I'm not one of them and don't ever plan to be.''

She smiled. With all of his gentle ways, Ben was a rebel at heart. When she'd been young, before her marriage to Amos, a part of her had wanted to rebel, too. Perhaps if she had met Ben then she would have found in him a kindred spirit.

Perhaps she had.

WHEN BECKY WOKE from her nap, Ben enticed her into a game of Frisbee before going into town for their promised ice cream.

"Come on, Sarah," he cajoled. "You, too."

"You two go ahead. I'll just clean up our lunch things."

Ignoring her objection, he snared her hands and pulled Sarah to her feet. "It's more fun with three."

She gasped and felt herself flushing. "Really, Ben, a married woman needs to show a little dignity."

"But you aren't married," he said pointedly. "Not anymore."

"I'm Becky's mother. It's the same thing."

He arched a brow. "Meaning, you're not allowed to have any fun?"

His challenge pricked whatever sense of rebellion remained in her. Snatching the Frisbee from his hand, she skipped back out of his reach. "It means women are better at throwing Frisbees than men are, and we're reluctant to damage their male egos. But if you insist—" She spun the flying saucer at him with all her might, and he leaped into the air, skirt flying, to snare it.

"All right, woman! If that's how you want to play the game." The red disc came spinning back to her, sailing over her head.

"My turn, my turn!" Becky demanded, laughing at their antics.

Before long they were all laughing. Not allowed to run yet because of her surgery, Becky had both Ben and Sarah chasing the wayward Frisbee from one side of the open meadow to the other. It did Sarah's heart good to see Becky so happy and carefree, particularly after the fright of her appendix nearly bursting. She registered another emotion, too, one she was reluctant to admit. It had been a very long time since Sarah had had this much fun. And it was Ben who was responsible for the feeling.

The shadow of the cottonwood trees stretched out across the meadow as the afternoon sped by.

"If we're going to get home for supper, we'd better leave now," Sarah warned.

"We've still gotta do ice cream," Ben said.

"It will spoil Becky's dinner."

"Uh-uh," the child protested. "I'll even eat my peas, I promise."

With a defeated shake of her head and a smile, Sarah said, "I guess once won't hurt."

"Yeah for mom!" Ben shouted, and gave his little girl a high five.

Ben packed up the picnic basket, placing it in the back of the buggy, while Sarah harnessed the horse—a skill Ben had never acquired. He hefted

Becky onto the front seat and swung up beside her. Sarah took the reins.

Settling between the two grown-ups, Becky asked, "Fannie, how come sometimes your voice is real deep?" She lowered her voice to mimic his. "And sometimes it's *real, real* high," she squeaked.

His head snapped down to look at her. So much for forgetting his masquerade. "Guess I've got kind of a scratchy throat."

Her forehead puckered and she didn't look convinced by his answer. "An' how come you wears boy's short pants under your dress?"

"Yeah, well...it's sort of the style where I come from." Kids asked too damn many questions.

"Is it somethin' I'm not s'posed to talk about?"

"That's right, honey." He needed a way to distract her, and he needed it in a hurry. "How 'bout we sing some songs?"

"Church songs?" she piped up.

He noted Sarah's lips quivering with the threat of a smile. She thought he'd been outmaneuvered by a pint-size kid because he hadn't known a single one of the hymns the Amish had sung at the church service he attended. "Maybe something a little livelier."

He searched his brain for a suitable song, one that would keep Becky's curious little mind occupied for a while. "Ninety-nine Bottles of Beer on the Wall" probably wouldn't win Sarah's approval, so he settled for a high-pitched rendition of "John Jacob Jingleheimer Schmidt." They had reached the whispered chorus by the time they turned on to the main street of Peacock.

Tourists gawked at them as Sarah manuevered the buggy through heavy traffic. One guy came running out from the sidewalk to snap their picture with a cheap instamatic. Sarah averted her face.

"What's the matter with these people?" Ben grumbled. "Don't they know the Amish don't like to have their pictures taken?"

"They're curious about us is all," Sarah said. "They mean us no harm."

Ben considered going after the guy with the camera, ripping out the film and exposing it. He also gave some thought to paying the man for the film so he'd have a picture of Sarah. Neither choice seemed exactly in character while he was dressed like an Amish woman.

Becky squirmed on the seat to look back over her shoulder. "I don't care if they take my picture."

"If you were a grown woman, it would show conceit to have a picture made," Sarah said, gently reminding her daughter of their beliefs.

Looking guilty, Becky glanced at Ben. All he could do was shrug. It wasn't his place to correct her mother, even if he couldn't see anything wrong with having a picture taken. A lot of the Amish beliefs didn't make sense to him, and that provided the real crux of his dilemma. Would Sarah be willing to give all of that up for him?

Sarah parked the rig in a vacant lot near the ice cream store, and they walked the rest of the way.

"Usually there's a man with me when I come to town—one of my stepsons," Sarah said. "The tourists stare less then."

"You'd get a second look from me anytime, anyplace," Ben confided, leaning toward her so Becky wouldn't hear. "You are picture perfect."

The color of sunrise stole into her peaches-and-cream cheeks. "Hush!" she ordered, but he noted a pleased smile curling her lips.

They waited while a group of senior citizens got their ice cream, then Ben ordered. "She'll have a double peppermint stick cone and I'll have chocolate. What do you want, Miss Muffet?"

She peered wide-eyed into the refrigerator display case and licked her lips. "Chocolate's best."

The pimply-faced clerk passed the cones over the counter. "That'll be three seventy-five."

Ben reached for his wallet.

The bell on the store's front door jangled as another group of tourists entered, crowding up to the counter.

Ah, hell! His wallet was in the hip pocket of his jeans—under his dress!

He handed Sarah his cone. "I'll be right back."

"What's wrong?"

"I can't get to my wallet," he hissed between clenched teeth. "Not in front of all these people."

Her eyes widened and she bit back a smile. "I can buy—"

"No, this is my treat."

"You don't have to—"

He shoved through a swinging gate that led to the back room.

"Ma'am, you can't go in there," the clerk complained. "Please, ma'am—"

Ben was going to "ma'am" the kid right in his teeth if he didn't shut up. Hiking up his skirt, he whipped out his wallet and grabbed a five-dollar bill. He marched out of the storeroom and slapped it on the counter. "Keep the change."

By the time they were back on the sidewalk, Sarah was laughing so hard that Ben could have strangled her. Or kissed her. He like that idea better.

"What's so funny, Mama?"

"Nothing, Becky, it's just that your mama—" She choked on another spasm of giggles. She wiped her eyes with the handful of napkins she'd taken from the ice cream shop. "I'm sorry."

"Yeah, well…" In spite of himself, Ben grinned. There was nothing he enjoyed more than to see Sarah happy. If that caused him a few embarrassing moments, it was damn well worth it.

When they reached the buggy, she stopped and a frown replaced the smile on her face. "How did you know I like peppermint ice cream?"

"We spent one whole Sunday afternoon looking for someplace that carried that flavor. I guess you were feeling homesick."

In a gesture so sweet that it brought tears to his eyes, she palmed his face. "*Danke,* Ben. For the ice cream and our picnic. This day has made me very happy."

That was all the thanks he needed—to make her

happy. He wanted to spend the rest of his life doing just that.

ON THE WAY HOME, they didn't talk much, just ate their ice cream. When Sarah pulled the rig into the farmyard, they discovered another buggy parked out front.

"Who's here?" Ben asked.

A gaggle of kids came running out from behind the house, waving at Sarah.

"Samuel and his family have come to visit," Sarah said stoically, drawing the buggy to a halt. Her face had turned to a mask, every spark of pleasure from the afternoon gone. "The man I will marry soon after the harvest is in."

The ice cream in Ben's stomach curdled, and reality hit him full force. Today had meant nothing to her.

She was still planning to marry someone else.

Chapter Nine

Only steps behind his children, Samuel appeared, his strides long, his expression dour. His straw hat sat squarely on his head, the brim the perfect width prescribed by the church, his white shirt pocketless, for a pocket might be construed as ornamentation. A leader in the church, there'd be no fear that Samuel Mast would leave the settlement, destroying his family in the process or placing them in jeopardy of shunning.

A safe man.

Sarah's chest tightened with guilt. Her day with Ben had been a frivolous interlude. For a time, she'd forgotten her responsibilities, the promises she'd vowed to keep. Little wonder they called her Forgetful Sarah.

Samuel took the bridle, controlling the horse, and Sarah climbed down from the buggy into the gathering of youngsters. Samuel's youngest, two-year-old Tess, lifted her arms to be picked up. With a smile, Sarah complied, happy to have the distraction. Though a stern man and a hard taskmaster—

as Amos had been—Samuel had raised three beautiful children. Not only were they easy to love, but she sensed they needed a woman's gentle touch.

"Where have you been?" Samuel asked. His gaze flicked suspiciously toward Fannie, who was helping Becky out of the buggy.

Instinctively, as she would with any child, Sarah hugged Tess, kissing her cheek. With her free hand she ruffled the dark hair of the two older youngsters—Joshua, the same age as Becky, and Abe, now eight. The children would be hers to raise after her marriage to their father, and she looked forward to the responsibility, and the happiness of a growing family. "We picnicked by the creek."

He raised his eyebrows in surprise. "On a weekday?"

"The chores were done," she said defensively, bristling at Samuel's implied criticism. She was a good mother and conscientious in her work. She canned the vegetables she grew in her garden, cleaned and baked, took food to the sick, scrubbed and kept her house spotless, and cared for her child. Yet Samuel apparently thought that was not enough. She fumed at his mild censure—and her need to make an excuse for a rare day of play.

"Fannie had not yet seen our countryside."

"I thought the healer was supposed to be teaching you medicinal cures, *ja?* Not gallivanting all over the neighborhood."

Her rarely aroused temper came to a slow boil. She opened her mouth to respond, but Ben stepped up to Samuel. He stood wide-legged, his hands on his hips. In a panic, Sarah thought surely Samuel would see through Ben's disguise, particularly since his cap only partially covered his long hair.

"The lady needed a day off," Ben said, his high-pitched voice incongruous given his aggressive stance.

"Let's go inside where it's cooler?" she hastily urged, secretly pleased with Ben's defense of her. Lowering Tess to the ground, she took the child's hand. "I'm sure the children would like some lemonade."

"*Ja! Ja!*" they chorused, racing for the front porch, Becky leading the way. Tess escaped Sarah's grip to toddle along behind them.

Samuel and Ben eyed each other like two bulls in a pasture with only one cow. Or at least that's how it seemed to Sarah, and she flushed. Never before had any man displayed jealousy on her account, or even possessiveness, though she quickly chided herself for enjoying the moment. Pride was not a trait to be encouraged in oneself.

"Samuel, would you put up my horse in the barn while Fannie and I fix the lemonade?" she asked, hoping to separate the two men before they came to blows. Ben, she suspected, was fully capable of violence if provoked. Samuel, a man of peace, would be no match for him.

"The hinges on your barn door are coming loose," Samuel said, speaking to Sarah but not taking his eyes off Ben. Suspicion darkened his eyes and rode heavily on his brows. "If you had told me, I would have fixed them."

"I was going to ask one of the boys—"

"I'll do it when we come to harvest your fields at the end of the week."

Sarah's breath caught. "So soon?" She'd thought there'd be more time before the harvest— and her wedding that would soon follow.

"That's what I came by to tell you. The corn's near full ripe. To wait longer would mean risking the crop. The weather could change."

"Yes, of course." A successful farmer like Samuel would know best, but Sarah wished there were some way to delay the inevitable. "Well, come in then and rest a while."

He shot Ben another look that could only be described as antagonistic. "I've no time to waste like some others do. I'll get my young'uns, and we'll be on our way."

"*Ach,* leave the children, Samuel," she suggested, trying to smooth his ruffled feathers. "Becky has so few chances to play with her friends. I'll bring them home after supper."

He hesitated, still eyeing Ben.

"I promise not to feed them any rhubarb," Ben said with a strangely smug smile.

Sarah's eyebrows rose. *Rhubarb?*

Under his breath, Samuel muttered something that sounded shockingly like a curse, then he turned and marched to his own buggy, obviously forgetting Sarah had asked him to put up her horse.

Sarah pursed her lips. She had never seen Samuel act so out of sorts.

"That guy's a real grump," Ben said, as Samuel

drove his buggy up the lane. "Can't think why you'd want to marry him."

She frowned. Her husband-to-be had seemed unusually tense. While she might not feel any romantic spark between them, she was sure he'd be an excellent husband and provider. "Samuel's usually very nice, and his children are adorable. Perhaps his stomach is bothering him today. A little indigestion, maybe?"

Winking at her, Ben grinned and said, "Nope, it's his spleen."

With that, he led Sarah's horse and buggy to the barn. For a man who made his living in the construction trade, Sarah marveled that he was so quickly learning the skills needed on a farm.

But why would he think Samuel's spleen was acting up? And be so tickled about it?

Puzzled, Sarah shook her head and went inside to prepare the promised lemonade for the children.

She recalled that when she was a young woman, the boys she'd gone to school with—those who might have courted her—had more often been leery of her than friendly. She'd made the mistake too often of having a sharp tongue or performing better than they did in school. So they'd kept their distance. She'd made them nervous.

During the years of her marriage she'd tried valiantly to curb her tongue and her wit. When she failed, her punishment involved days of silence from Amos. Guiltily, she realized that after a while she'd almost looked forward to those times.

But whatever intelligence she had didn't seem to

bother Ben. He laughed easily...and today he'd begun teaching her to laugh again, even when he and his outrageous costume were the brunt of the joke.

Pulling open the back door, she shuddered. When was the last time she'd heard the sound of Samuel's laughter? Or had she ever?

Which was not to say he was a mean man. He'd always been gentle with Becky and as kind to her as he was with his own children. But there seemed to be little in life that brought a smile to his face.

In contrast, she realized Ben smiled all of the time—and often made *her* laugh.

BEN'S VICTORY had been small and fleeting, he thought as he finished up in the barn. The fact that he could outsmart Samuel Mast didn't mean Sarah would change her mind about whom she'd marry.

In the kitchen, the kids were gathered around the table drinking their lemonade and eating homebaked chocolate chip cookies. Big fat crayons were scattered about, the youngsters coloring on plain sheets of white paper. Sarah looked at home, supervising the impromptu classroom of children who were not her own. Youngsters she wanted to mother.

Damn, but he wanted the children she mothered to be his. The way Becky was.

He chose a cookie from the plate in the middle of the table. "I fixed the hinges on the barn door."

She looked up from helping the youngest of the bunch. "*Danke,* Ben. I wondered what had kept you so long."

"The holes had gotten too big for the screws. I had to plug them and re-screw them. A power drill would have made the job faster."

"But no more appreciated." Her teasing smile reminded him that the Amish didn't use electricity and didn't value what it could do. In contrast, electric power made Ben's construction business possible.

"Look at me, Fannie," Becky cried. "I know my letters." Childishly scrawled capital letters from A to Z covered her paper.

"Hey, that's great, Miss Muffet." *Smart like her old man,* Ben thought with a grin.

"Josh can't even write his name yet. That means I'm smarter than him."

"Becky!" her mother admonished. "Remember, pride goeth before destruction."

"Well, it's true," Becky said, pouting. "I can even *read.*"

"I don't need to know dumb stuff like reading," Josh insisted. Crayoned purple stars of every possible size decorated his paper, and some of them had been doodled onto the tabletop. "My dad already lets me help him plow. Bet he won't let you. You're just a girl!"

"Girls are better than boys!"

"Are not!"

"Children, that's enough. In God's eyes you are all perfect creatures." Sarah rested a reassuring hand on each of the two adversaries, which seemed to reduce the antagonism for the moment. Admittedly she, too, was proud of her daughter's intelligence. But in an Amish community, all children were valued equally, and their academic achievement was of little note. Any child who attempted to lord it over another was quickly isolated from the group.

Cruelly ostracized, as Sarah well remembered.

All her life she'd been told to hold her tongue, or even to disguise the fact that she excelled in academics. She'd often failed in that endeavor. She'd loved school. Not being permitted to pursue an education beyond the eighth grade—all an Amish child was allowed—had been a bitter sacrifice for her. She'd wanted to have more knowledge of the world, so much so that from an early age she had considered running away. She'd wanted to become—

Her gaze shot to Ben. *She'd wanted to become a nurse.*

But she hadn't acted on that secret desire, she quickly amended. That would have been tantamount to leaving her family and destroying the only life she knew. Surely she hadn't been so foolish as to actually pursue that dream and suffer the guilt that would follow.

Her temple throbbed and an image popped into her mind. Vaguely she was aware of the children in her own kitchen, of Abe helping his younger brother with his letters. But what she saw in her mind's eye was quite different.

A classroom. Not the one-room schoolhouse where she'd studied as a child—very much like the one Becky would soon attend—but a roomful of adults. Standing in one corner of the room, like a youngster being punished for some misdeed, was a full-size skeleton. *Femur, patella, tibia, fibula,* she mentally chanted, giving names to the bones in the skeleton's legs.

Her hand flew to her mouth. Dear heaven, she had never learned that at her Amish school.

"What's wrong?" Ben asked.

The children at the table, engrossed in their own efforts, paid no attention to Ben—or to Sarah.

"I know the names of bones—human bones," she said in a shocked whisper, stunned by the revelation. "Clavicle, sternum, scapula and humerus."

"Sure you do. I helped you memorize them."

"But I couldn't possibly remember—"

He caught her chin between his thumb and forefinger, holding her in a gentle vise. In the muted light of the kitchen, his eyes were a deep blue, his gaze penetrating. His woman's garb no longer disguised his masculinity in her eyes, but enhanced it instead, the contrast so sharp that it made her heart thunder in her chest. "Nobody ever studied harder than you did. You can't have forgotten everything you learned."

"But that would mean—" Her whole world, everything she'd known and believed, tilted upside down. She had found a balance in her life. Now Ben, and her new memories, were destroying that. All but losing her equilibrium, she pulled away from him. "I need to talk to my parents."

"I'll go with you."

"Nein." She shook her head. "I need to do this by myself."

"I'm involved in this, too, Sarah. Your parents stole you away from me. As far as I'm concerned, they as good as kidnapped you."

"Let me talk to them first. They'll tell me the truth." Now, after all these years, surely they wouldn't keep such a desperate secret. They'd tell her what she'd been doing during the months Sarah had forgotten; they'd assure her she hadn't been living in sin, pregnant without the blessings of marriage.

Tess tugged on Sarah's skirt. "Pee-pee, Sarah," the child whispered.

"I can take her," Becky volunteered, eager to play at being big sister.

"No, I will." Sarah took the child's hand. She needed to get away from Ben, from what he made her feel and remember. Simply by being in her house, he undermined her equilibrium. Confused her. He was an outsider. She couldn't listen to him. For her own sake—and that of her child—she didn't *dare* listen to him.

Or be pleased by the fact he found some joy and pleasure in her ability to pursue academic subjects.

As Sarah hurried from the kitchen, Ben started to jam his hands in his pockets, then remembered that he was still wearing a fool skirt. How could he expect Sarah to react to him as she would to a man when he spent half his time masquerading as a women? When she looked at him, she probably saw a clown.

But she had been remembering something. Her love of learning could be the key to unlocking her amnesia.

"I've gotta go make a phone call," he told the remaining kids at the kitchen table. "Tell Sarah I'll be right back."

At the phone booth by the road, Ben lifted his skirt and pulled his wallet from his pocket. Using his credit card, he placed a call to his partner, Mac Culdane, and told him succinctly what he needed.

"Can't you give me a day or two?" Mac complained. "Without you here things are a little crazy. This weekend—"

"Sorry, Mac. I don't have much time left. If I don't act now, I'm going to lose Sarah again. I'll make it up to you, Mac. I swear I will." His throat tight with fear, Ben glanced toward Sarah's house, caught now in the lengthening shadows of evening. "I don't care how much it costs, Mac. Use a special messenger if you have to, but I need the stuff tonight."

There was a lengthy pause on the other end of the phone. "Your Sarah has got to be one special lady for you to go to all this trouble, son."

"She is."

"You can count on me. I'll get you want you need—if I have to bring it down there myself."

Ben tried to say thanks but his throat was too clogged with emotion. He could only hope his plan worked.

IT WAS PAST NINE that evening when the messenger showed up at the door. Sarah had taken Samuel's children home hours ago and then escaped upstairs with Becky, pleading fatigue. She just didn't want to face Ben, and he knew it. He also wasn't going to let Sarah get away with that. She was going to deal with him. Now. And this time she'd see him as a man, the dress he had been wearing stashed upstairs in his bedroom when he'd changed an hour ago.

"Hey, man, I thought I'd never find this place. Don't any of you people believe in porch lights?" The scrawny twenty-year-old special messenger handed Ben the package he'd been expecting.

"No, they don't." Pulling his wallet from his back pocket, he slipped out a couple of twenties. "This oughta make up for your trouble."

The young man's eyes bulged. "Hey, yeah, man. That's great. No problem. Anytime at all."

Ben closed the door.

As he walked upstairs, he organized his thoughts. Or tried to. Mostly he was an emotional basket case. If he messed up in the next few days, he'd lose Sarah—and Becky—forever.

FROM HER UPSTAIRS WINDOW, Sarah saw a car drive away from the house. A moment later she heard a soft rap on her bedroom door. *"Ja?"*

Her breath caught when Ben stepped into the room. His white T-shirt stretched snugly across his chest, defining well-developed muscles and emphasizing a flat belly; his stone-washed, cut-off jeans rode unfairly low, gloving lean hips. While he had been garbed in his Amish dress, she could almost disregard how totally, overwhelmingly masculine he was. How much of an outsider he was to her Amish traditions.

Dressed as he was now, and as he had been most evenings recently when they were alone, there was little of his physique left to her imagination. His tight-fitting jeans strained at the telltale zipper, leaving the impression that he was a big man in every way conceivable.

Wrapping her arms around her midsection, she was shockingly aware that she wore only a plain cotton nightgown, far more revealing than the voluminous dress and concealing apron of a proper Amish woman. She'd just brushed her hair, and it hung loose nearly to her waist, uncut—as was the custom of her people.

Instinctively, Sarah backed toward the far corner of the room. This man was more dangerous than the one she'd come to know as Fannie—even when dressed in cut-offs. That person had been gentle. While not threatening, this man was overpowering simply by being in her bedroom. He seemed to fill the space, consuming the air, leaving her breathless.

"When it's just the two of us, I don't see any reason to keep up the masquerade," he said.

"I know but Becky might—"

"She's sound asleep. Besides, it's high time you start thinking of me as a man."

She swallowed hard. "I know you're a man." How could she help but know? Every inch of him spoke to her of forbidden things, of kisses and caresses and intimate passions she had only dreamed about.

"Do you?" His gaze slid to the bed that stood between them and the quilt she'd turned back, almost as if it were an invitation.

"Of course I do." Defensively, she pulled the bedding back into place. "What is it you wanted?"

"Now that's a question with only one good answer," he drawled. One corner of his mouth hooked up in a teasing smile.

Her heart rate accelerated and her face flushed as a shocking burst of desire blossomed low in her body. Ben wouldn't take her *against* her will, she was sure. But the titillating possibility that it wouldn't be against her will made her mouth go dry. She licked her lips. "I heard a car."

"Yeah. A delivery I'd been expecting."

Only then did she realize he'd been carrying a package wrapped in brown paper. As brazen as you please, he fluffed the pillow on the far side of the double bed and tossed back the quilt.

"What are you doing?" she gasped. Her heart thrust uncomfortably hard against her breastbone.

"You used to like to study in bed." He stretched out, propping himself on the pillow, and patted the bed beside him.

Her insides clinched. "You'd better leave."

"Not till you see what's in the package." With suggestive slowness, he ripped off one corner of the paper, revealing the edge of a hardbound book. "Let me see. Looks like this one is algebra. Math wasn't your favorite subject. I had to tutor you some, but you caught on pretty fast.''

"I never took any such class!"

"It was required to get into nurses' training." He set that book aside and slid another one from the wrapper. "You liked this better—*Human Anatomy.* You said you had to memorize every word in this book if you were going to be a good nurse. I used to drill you for hours on end. You got an *A* on your midterm.''

"Where did you get those books?"

"I called my partner, Mac Culdane. He's got a key to my house, and I had him stop by."

"Why would you have these books at your house? And they certainly have nothing to do with me.''

"They were *your* books, Sarah. All this time, I never had the heart to throw them away. I thought you might come back."

He was mistaken, of course. Even so, Sarah's heart tightened at the sweetness of the gesture, however misguided. Maybe somewhere in this world she had a secret twin. A double. Or perhaps she was simply going crazy.

"Now this one," he said, holding up a heavy volume, "is the one I asked my partner to pick up for you at the bookstore today. It's called *A Layman's Guide to Family Medicine.* Wanna take a look?"

"Oh, my..." Unable to resist, she reached for the book.

He snatched it back. "No, you don't." He patted

the bed beside him again. "To get a look at this little puppy you have to join me."

She bristled. "I'm not going to sleep with you simply because—"

"Who said anything about sleeping? We're going to study it together. After all, I'm supposed to be teaching you medical stuff."

"That's ridiculous! I mean, it's very kind of you to get me the book—" and very tempting, too "—but I'm not going to lie down with you. It's not…it's not *proper.*"

"Okay, we'll try it another way." In a flash, he was on his feet, rolling the quilt into a long barricade he stretched down the length of the bed. "We'll try bundling."

"Bund—ling?" Her voice hitched.

"Sure. It's an old Amish custom."

"It is no such thing. Or at least, it hasn't been in this century."

"Then we'll bring it back. Start a new fad." His arrogant grin rankled as much as it sped up her heart rate.

"When people actually *did* bundle, they did it because it was the dead of winter and the houses weren't heated. They had to get under the covers so they wouldn't freeze. In case you haven't noticed, it's still very much summer."

"So we'll fake the freezing part." He plopped down on the bed again and crooked his finger at her. "I swear, I won't cross the line. Come on. What can it hurt? And you know you're curious about these books.'' He held one book up, waggling it.

She was curious, insatiable for new knowledge. More than she cared to admit. ''Not the algebra book,'' she hedged, almost salivating to get her hands on the medical guide. With the information in that book she might be able to help her friends and neighbors should they become ill, and that had been her lifelong goal. *A goal important enough that she might once have run away in pursuit of that learning,* an irritating voice in her head taunted.

''Okay, we'll skip the math for now.'' He grinned at her—that irresistible smile that dimpled his cheek—and patted the bed one more time.

''You promise to stay on your own side?''

''Cross my heart.''

Gingerly, keeping herself as far away from Ben as she could, she stretched out on the bed. The kerosene lamp on the bed table flickered, sending shadows dancing across the room. Unbidden, desire fluttered low in her abdomen again and she tamped it down.

His gaze never leaving her face, Ben passed her the book. ''There you go. That wasn't so painful, was it?''

Oh, yes it was. Her heart beat so hard that it filled her throat, making breathing difficult. The mere thought of lying in the same bed with Ben made her limbs feel weak. Actually doing it, suspecting she had done this before, made her head spin.

Dear heaven! If she'd made love with this man,

how could she possibly have forgotten? The memory would be permanently etched in her brain, something she'd carry with her to her grave.

Taking the book, she forced herself to open it, to concentrate on the pages as she flipped through them. Forced herself not to think about Ben kissing her. Taking her in his arms. Loving her. Ignoring such thoughts was made all the more difficult by the way Ben toyed with the tips of her hair, running the strands through his fingers.

The air in the room grew hot and expectant. Beneath her nightgown, her skin became overly sensitive, aware of the cotton fabric skimming her breasts and the way her body sank in the softness of the mattress.

She trembled, her hands shaking. She tried to draw a steadying breath, but found the air too thick to slip past the constriction in her throat.

"This is very nice," she said, handing him back the book and shifting her hair away from him. "But I think you'd better go now." If he stayed, she'd do terrible things.

Wonderful things.

"The book's for you, Sarah. A gift."

Something precious to hold on to, something beyond value, a reminder of Ben to cling to after he'd gone—and someday soon, he *would* have to leave. Gifts were rare among the Amish and always simple. A book like this was a treasure, more appreciated by Sarah than another woman—an outsider—would value the most precious jewels.

"*Danke*, Benjamin," she whispered.

"You're welcome." Raising himself up on his elbow, he leaned over the folded quilt—their bundling board—and lowered his head towards hers. Crossing the line.

"You promised…"

But he didn't stop. His lips found hers, familiar now in the way they stole her breath away. But there was more. His fingers slipping through the hair that she'd brushed free only minutes ago, he kneaded her scalp, sending a shiver of sensual pleasure through her. And longing. A soft moan escaped her. Lust tugged at her good reason as his distinctive flavor filled her, his musky scent enveloped her.

In spite of herself, she hooked her hand around his nape, her fingers threading through his silken hair as his did through hers. She pulled him closer. A flame burned low in her belly.

Tempted, she bargained with her conscience. To feel just once the passion his touch promised would not be so awful. Later, she could beg forgiveness. She'd know, then, what pleasure had eluded her all those years in her marriage bed.

Slowly, in deliberate exploration, she let her tongue tease with his. The kiss grew hotter, his seduction wilder as he angled his mouth against hers again, boldly accepting what she had offered. His hand slipped down her throat, caressing a fevered path until it closed over her breast.

Her eyes flew open and she gasped. "Ben!"

"It's all right, love."

"No!" Oh, she wanted it to be all right, but her

conscience had refused the bargain. She couldn't do this. Not with a man who was not her husband. "You promised!"

"I'm not a saint, Sarah. I want you too much."

She scrambled off the bed. "Please go."

He drew a few deep breaths, and she knew how much it cost him to comply with her demand. "Enjoy your reading." He rolled off the bed, tucking his T-shirt into his jeans. "I've gotta say, bundling is a hell of a lot harder on a guy than I expected."

He left the room, and Sarah stared for a long time at the door that had closed behind him. She wanted to go after him; she didn't dare.

Rousing herself, she picked up the medical guide again and flipped through the pages. Diagrams of the human body blurred with pages of symptoms and ways to distinguish chicken pox from measles or an ordinary rash. Some details were common knowledge, but all of the information would be useful—once she was able to focus on the explanations.

So restless she was unable to even consider sleep, she picked up the anatomy book. As she opened it, a sheet of lined paper slipped out. Unfolding it, she studied the handwritten list of bones in the human body. A test, she realized.

Her lips pursed, and she stared in disbelief.

The handwriting was unquestionably hers, the grade she'd received an *A*.

Her hands shaking, she flipped open the book to the first page—where she had written her own name. And the date...six years ago.

Benjamin Miller hadn't lied to her. The book he'd had delivered had once belonged to her. She'd been studying to be a nurse. She had been living with him or he wouldn't have had her book. A book he'd saved because he'd hoped she would return to him.

A confusion of emotions filled her as she picked up the plain wrapping paper, only to have a yard of brightly colored silk fabric slip into her hand. The material spilled out as lightly as cottonwood seeds floating above a creek, the pattern of the scarf as bright as spring flowers massed on a hillside.

Dear heaven, this had been Ben's gift, too, the one he had spoken of. And she had forgotten.

Tears burned at the back of her eyes. Why couldn't she remember? Why had her parents kept Ben a secret from her?

And what else did they know that they hadn't told her?

Chapter Ten

"But you must have had some idea of what I'd been doing, Mother."

"We only knew you had run away—our first-born child—breaking our hearts. The hospital called Gordon Smith in town. He drove out to tell us you'd been hurt and you told them we were your family. All that mattered to your father and me was that we had a chance to bring you back home where you belonged."

"So you snatched me out of the hospital when I was barely conscious without telling me I'd been in a motorcycle accident with a man? An outsider?"

"The bishop assured us the details of your time away weren't important. We had you home again. Everything else could be forgiven."

Forgiven? Sarah paced the floor of the kitchen where she'd spent so much of her childhood, and wondered if she would find it in her heart to forgive her parents for keeping so many secrets from her.

Or to forgive herself for not having pressed for answers years ago.

Her parents, Elsa and Mordicah Lapp, lived two hours by buggy from Sarah's home. Leaving Becky with Ben, she'd driven the rig here alone this morning, determined to seek the truth. From the moment she had set foot in the farmhouse where she'd been raised, feelings of impotence washed over her. There was no way to argue with her parents, her father particularly was always *right,* no matter what anyone else said.

"What if that man had been important to me?" Sarah asked her mother. *What if I had loved him and had forgotten that love?*

Elsa Lapp waved off the possibility as though it had no credence. In middle age, her blond hair had begun to gray and her pale blue eyes were bracketed with wrinkles; her narrow lips formed a perpetually dour line. "You were to marry Amos Yoder."

"I don't remember ever agreeing to such a thing before I left home. Before the accident." She barely recalled knowing Amos *before* their wedding day.

"So you forgot. Why complain now? He gave you a good life and you had his baby."

"Are you sure, Mama? *Is* Becky Amos's child? Or could some other man be her father?"

Elsa's eyes widened in shock and she paled. "How can you say such a thing? I raised you to be a good girl. You never would have—"

"Did the hospital tell you I was pregnant? Is that why you married me off to Amos before I came to my senses? I'd had a concussion, Mama. I hardly knew what I was doing.''

"*Nein, nein!* What a terrible thing to think. Papa and I, we wanted you settled down, married to a good Amish man. You were our baby, and we'd lost so many others. I couldn't bear..." Her voiced failed her, and she sobbed. "My babies..."

"Oh, Mama." Sarah took her mother in her arms. "But what if there'd been another man? Someone I loved." A man who had spent years tracking her down, a man she couldn't remember.

"We only did what we thought was right. If you had stayed with the outsider, we never would have seen you again. Never."

"But I *was* with him, wasn't I, Mama? When I had the accident."

"We didn't know for sure how you knew this man. Only that you were riding on his motorcycle when he crashed. He might have been a stranger. We couldn't know for sure."

But surely they had sensed there was something more or they wouldn't have checked Sarah out of the hospital in such haste—while Ben was still unconscious. "You and Papa had no right to keep him a secret from me."

"We had *every* right. You are our daughter."

Sarah whirled at the sound of her father's voice. He'd come in from his chores for his noon meal, his shirt and the band of his straw hat sweaty from a morning's work.

"But, Papa—"

"We protected you from your own foolishness.

That is all you need to know. The rest is well forgotten.'' Sitting down at the table, he silently ordered his wife to bring his meal.

Elsa hurried to do his bidding, retrieving the leftovers of a roast from the refrigerator. She cut thick slices and served them with big slabs of homemade brown bread.

Taking the chair opposite her father—the one she had sat in as a child—Sarah let him sate his appetite before she began her questions again. In Amish households, conversation at mealtime was often limited to which farm chore should be accomplished next. Silence reigned—particularly among the children if they knew what was good for them.

To her surprise, she realized dinnertime conversation with Ben was relaxed, not tense as it had been with Amos or in her own family. What a strange custom it was not to speak to each other during meals, which often was the only time the entire family was together. Becky had always had some news of her day that she'd wanted to share with Amos, and so had his sons, but Sarah had been forced to silence them all. Later, by the time the opportunity came again to speak, all spontaneity had been lost.

In fact, in the short time Ben had been there, he had developed far more of a loving relationship with Becky than Amos ever had. They seemed to truly enjoy each other's company. Of course, Becky still thought of Fannie as a woman....

But discovering the truth about his masculinity had not changed the ease with which Sarah conversed with him, nor probably, would it change Becky's feelings.

What few conversations Sarah had shared with her own father had left her feeling vaguely guilty, as though she were to blame for having survived when her brothers had died. Shamefully, she still felt that way.

She leaned forward. "Papa, I need to know—"

"Not now, daughter." He drank from the glass of milk his wife had delivered to his place.

"*Ja,* Papa, *now!* Did you talk to the doctors about me?"

His bushy eyebrows lowering, he glared at her. "They said you were well enough to travel. That was all I needed to know."

"Did they tell you I was…going to have a baby?" She held her breath, waiting for his response.

He shoved back his chair, leaving his meal half eaten. "They told me no such thing. Go home, daughter. Marry Samuel Mast and do your duty by him."

"But if there's someone who—"

But he didn't wait for her to finish. Instead, without further conversation, he left by the back door.

Sarah lowered her head. She'd come for answers and there were none to be had. At least, not the ones she had hoped for, she realized. Blessings she needed aplenty. Instead she'd been granted another dose of guilt. To her dismay, the fear of bringing shame on her parents was as powerful a whip now as it had been in her youth.

Where on earth had she ever found the courage to run away?

Her mother's hand covered Sarah's shoulder. "It's my fault," she said.

Sarah glanced up. "Your fault?"

"When you were young, I gave you ideas. I'd lost my other babies and could have no more. You were all I had. I had too much pride in you, you were so smart. Smarter than the other children in the neighborhood. I was wrong to encourage you."

"You wanted me to be a nurse?"

"I wanted you happy. But I'd lost my babies—" Her voice caught, and she looked away.

Standing, Sarah framed her mother's face with her hands. "You hoped I could save other babies, didn't you?"

Elsa nodded. "It was my weakness—"

"Mama, do you know if I was pregnant when I had that accident?"

"Your papa talked to the doctor. He and I had hardly spoken since you'd run away. He said it was my fault. *My* pride that had led you to become an outsider."

"Don't blame yourself, Mama. It's what I wanted, too." Swallowing her own tears, Sarah hugged her mother. Though she hadn't found the answers she sought, she had found the source of her inspiration. But had too much time passed now for her to rebel again? Because now, throwing over the traces of the only life she knew and could remember would affect her child as well. And Becky was her life! Like her own mother, Sarah would do anything to protect her child.

Did she have the wisdom to know what was best for her daughter?

BEN TOOK THE BOARD he'd sawed to length and placed it across the risers of the back steps. "Okay, Becky, let's get this last one nailed in place before your mom gets home."

"How many nails do you want?"

"Hmm, how 'bout sixteen?" Ben grinned. The number wasn't as important as Becky's chance to show off her counting skills.

He waited patiently as she counted out the nails. With Becky's help, the job of repairing and replacing the back steps had probably taken twice as long as it might have otherwise. He didn't care. Nobody had ever had a more enthusiastic apprentice.

It had cost him plenty to leave Sarah's room last night, and see her go off to visit her folks this morning. He'd needed the distraction of doing something with his hands while he waited for her to return. Fixing the steps at least kept his mind occupied, instead of thinking how easy it would have been to cross that bundling line. He didn't think Sarah would have stopped him if he'd pressed the issue—she had responded to him. But guilt would have made her regret it this morning.

Ben didn't want it to be that way between them. He wanted Sarah to come willingly into his arms, into his life. And he was damn well going to stay out of her bed from now on, unless he was invited. Or so he told himself.

Delivering the handful of nails, Becky squatted down next to Ben. "My papa used to build things."

"You mean Amos?" *He wasn't your papa. I am,* he wanted to shout.

"Uh-huh. But he didn't want me underfoot."

"I like you just fine under my feet." In mock attack, he tapped his shoe lightly on top of her bare toes.

She squealed and danced away.

He laughed. Centering a nail, he hit it home with two sharp strokes, then picked up the next. He'd missed a lot by not having a chance to see Becky grow up. From now on, he wanted to be a part of her life. He could only hope Sarah would allow that to happen, that she'd be part of his life, too.

The sound of a horse and buggy approaching banished his thoughts. "Mama's home! Mama's home!" Becky went racing toward the front of the house just as Sarah's rig appeared.

"Careful, honey," Ben called. "Don't spook the horse." But Becky knew more about horses than he did. She skirted the animal and scrambled up into the buggy as soon as it came to a halt, claiming a hug from her mother.

Ben wished he could do the same. All day he'd been worried about what her parents would tell her. Would they lie? Would they send out the Amish equivalent of the cops to throw him off Sarah's farm?

"You've been busy," she said, eyeing his handiwork.

"You had some wood rot. I didn't want anyone to fall if a step gave way."

"*Danke,* Ben."

"I helped him, Mama. I helped him lots!"

Only a faint trace of a smile lifted Sarah's lips. "I'm sure you did."

Ben got a really bad feeling in the pit of his stomach. "Hey, Miss Muffet, how 'bout you putting away the hammer for me. You know where it goes?"

"*Ja.* I'm not a baby!" She scooped up the hammer from the steps.

"Walk—don't run with that," Ben reminded her as the child headed for the barn.

He turned to Sarah. "What did your folks say?"

She shook her head. "They denied knowing that you and I had lived together. Or even knew each other. Or that I was…pregnant."

His teeth clenched. "Do you believe them?"

"Who am I supposed to believe, Ben? My parents, who have always loved and cared for me? Or you, a stranger?"

"How about believing what you've seen with your own eyes? The books I brought you. The scarf you wore. The fact that I'm here, for God's sake."

"I don't know what to say." Tears sprang to her eyes and her chin quivered. "I remember bits and pieces of that time. That gang of hoodlums. Someone on a motorcycle. I thought it was all a dream. I remember going to a class. But I don't remember you, Ben. I'm sorry. As hard as I try, I can't seem to remember *you*."

Ben's heart was breaking. For him, Sarah was the dream; losing her, the nightmare. He wanted her, in the flesh, beside him when he woke up each morning.

Desperate, he framed her face with his hands. "Listen to me, sweetheart. Simply because you can't remember me doesn't mean that I'm lying about us. Why else would I have gone to all the trouble to find you if what I've told you isn't the truth? If I didn't love you?"

"I don't know, Ben. I simply don't know." She turned and walked away from him.

THOUGH SARAH SPENT a good deal of time worrying over that question, she still did not have the answer three days later when the harvesting began. She did know that she liked having Ben at her dinner table, discussing the day's events and laughing with Becky. And secretly she wished he had returned to her bedroom to bundle and kiss her again. With a sigh, she realized that particular longing made it abundantly clear that she hadn't a lick of wisdom at all.

Samuel was driving the team of horses for the corn-picking wagon, the machinery roaring as ears, stalks and tassels were slashed from the ground and scooped up into the bed of the collecting wagon driven by her stepson Thomas. As one wagon filled, another appeared in its place, Ely moving it into position. Behind the procession, her youngest stepson, John, Fannie and little Abe picked up the leavings.

The hot air was heavy with the sharp scent of dust and fresh-cut corn.

She smiled and rolled her eyes at the sight of Ben clopping through the field behind the wagons, his lopsided breasts off-center beneath the bib apron he wore. How much longer could his masquerade go undetected?

She shuddered to think what would happen if the charade was discovered. Samuel, she knew, would not be at all tolerant about a man living in Sarah's house.

Certainly her father would be furious if he learned about Ben's presence.

If only she could persuade Ben to leave before that happened. But he seemed determined to remain until she forced him to stand by his vow. *Until my marriage to Samuel.*

She swallowed hard. A week next Sunday would see the end of her indecision.

Envious of those who could participate in the harvest, the younger children ran around the yard, pretending they had the skills to be a farmer. They'd tried Tess as the team of horses to pull their little red wagon, but she couldn't budge it when either Josh or Becky were onboard. So naturally, Becky insisted Josh pull the wagon and she be the farmer. That resulted in another squabble, which nearly came to blows—instigated by Sarah's daughter.

Lord help her! What was she going to do with

these two youngsters when they were living under the same roof? She could only hope when they entered school next week that the influence of their classmates would calm their rivalry. And perhaps Becky would realize she must mind her manners if she was to be accepted by her peers.

The field was nearly half harvested when Samuel stopped for the noon meal. Sarah had everything ready, spread on a table in the shade of an elm in the front yard.

Ben was the last to wash up before sitting down to eat. In spite of herself, Sarah lingered near the pump, simply to be near him.

He dashed a handful of water into his sweat-streaked face. "Tell me this, Sweet Sarah." He wiped his face with a towel and dried his hands. "What's the logic of having a gas-powered corn-picker and using a horse-drawn wagon? Why don't you people just buy a tractor?"

"Because then we'd have to go into debt to buy the tractor. Then we would have to purchase more land to plant so we could harvest more corn so we could pay back all the loans we'd been forced to take out in order to expand the farm."

His lips twitched. "Okay. I asked for a logical reason and I guess that's what I got. But it sure seems peculiar reasoning to me."

"Our ways keep us closer to the land. We are content."

"Are you?"

This was a difficult question to answer. Yes,

she'd been content these past few years. *But at what cost?* she wondered as he headed for the table.

"Psst! Ben…" He turned and she gestured to his ill-formed figure. "You need to fix your, ah…"

He looked down, cursed softly and straightened his costume.

Sarah repressed a smile. How thoroughly self-confident he was as a man not to feel threatened by wearing such an outrageous disguise. She doubted Samuel would be as cavalier about such a thing.

Nor would Samuel have gone to such lengths to find her, she realized, her heart constricting at the thought of the troubling reality of her relationship with the man she would soon marry. Not that she harbored many romantic notions after her years of marriage to Amos…but it would be nice to feel something more for her husband than dutiful respect.

She started for the table, too, but a buggy turned into the lane. Sarah squinted to see who her visitor was. Perhaps another pair of helping hands for Samuel—or another mouth to feed.

To her delight, it was Short Martha. Sarah went to meet her as she climbed down from the rig.

"You're just in time for supper," Sarah said, always pleased to see her friend.

"*Ach,* that's good. I'd heard Samuel was harvesting your fields today. Hope the men haven't had their dessert yet."

"*Nein.* They just sat down to eat."

From the back of the buggy, Martha retrieved a large baking dish covered with foil. "I've made

Samuel his favorite apple dumplings, my special recipe with maple syrup and extra cinnamon.''

''Sounds delicious. I didn't know—''

''Oh, *ja*, since he was a little boy this is his favorite. I gave his wife Tillie—bless her soul—the recipe, too.''

''That's wonderful. I hope you'll share it with me, too.'' In some ways, she knew as little of Samuel as she did of Ben, despite the fact that they had been neighbors for the past six years. But the Amish did not encourage a great deal of interaction between men and women in the congregation. They had separate responsibilities.

''Of course I'll give you the recipe.'' Martha glanced toward those eating at the shaded table. ''Fannie is still here?''

''Yes, he's—she's helping with the harvest today.''

Martha raised her brows. ''Better than having the healer help with cooking, *ja?*''

''Much,'' she agreed with a laugh, hoping Martha hadn't caught her slip of the tongue.

Martha carried the baking dish to the table. ''Here you are, Samuel. Like when we were children and you begged me to make apple dumplings. Remember?''

''*Ja*, little Martha. Remember it well, I do,'' he said, his laughter booming, his eyes alight with pleasure.

In a gesture so affectionate that Sarah would not have believed it if she had not seen it with her own eyes, Samuel hugged Martha. They were distant cousins, she knew, and their families were close. In contrast, Samuel had never shown any particular sentiment toward Sarah.

She'd made a pledge of marriage her father expected her to honor. And if she didn't, her father would carry some of the shame.

"Martha, Martha, come sit by me," Josh pleaded.

"Me! Me!" Tess echoed.

Showing no favorites, Martha squeezed in between the two children and gave them both a hug. Perhaps because of her short stature, Martha had a particular affinity for children, and her love for them was obvious.

Martha should have been a wife and mother, Sarah thought with affection, thinking men rarely knew what was best for them.

She joined the others at the table, her mind once again spiraling into confusion. Did she have a right, as Ben had said, to choose a destiny different from the one her father demanded of her?

Her gaze met his down the length of the table. The man who claimed to love her.

Dear heaven, how did she feel about him? He was the kindest, gentlest man she'd ever met—yet strong, too. And comfortable with himself. Were her feelings for him deep enough for her to give up the safety of her home and the life she'd known? Had she in the past felt for him a love that had endured all this time in the private recesses of her forgotten memories?

The throbbing began again at her temples. If only she could remember.

When Ben had brought her the books, she'd remembered the classroom where she'd studied. Simply by coming here, he'd aroused other memories of that time in her life, too—the past her father had hoped she'd forget.

Perhaps there was only one way she could be sure of her feelings for Ben.

But did she have the nerve to risk making intimate discoveries that could never again be forgotten?

IT WAS ALMOST DARK when the harvesting stopped for the day. The boys went home to Ely's house to eat and finish their chores, but Samuel and his children stayed at Sarah's for dinner.

"Samuel!" she called. "Children! Dinner's ready." She smiled at Ben, who'd been helping her in the kitchen—or trying to. She'd finally relegated him to chopping the vegetables for the salad. He'd worked so hard in the fields today, she wouldn't have asked for his help at all. But he'd insisted.

With thundering feet, the youngsters responded to her call, taking their places around the big dining table.

"Sarah!" Samuel called from the living room. "I need to see you."

Meeting Ben's frowning gaze, she shrugged. "Serve the children, *bitte*, please, and get them started. I'll see what he wants." How comfortable she felt asking for and receiving Ben's help for *any* chore, even one typically performed by a woman.

Smiling slightly, she followed the sound of Samuel's voice.

"What is this filthy book doing here?" he asked. His voice was low and taut as though he was trying valiantly to control his anger. He waved the medical guide in her face.

She bristled at his tone. Evidently she'd left Ben's gift lying on the end table where she'd been reading it last night. "It's a medical book. There's nothing dirty about—"

"There are pictures of naked men and women in here. You should give some thought to the children. Having this book—"

She snatched it away from him. "They are *sketches* of people, not pictures."

His weathered, angular features creased even more deeply. "It's the same thing. Their *genitals* are showing! I don't want my children seeing—"

"Oh, for heaven's sake, Samuel! The children live on a farm. They know something about—"

"I'll not have that book in my house, do you hear me? Burn it!"

"This isn't your house, and as we are not yet married, you have no right to give me orders. Furthermore, I intend to keep this book and study it for as long as I like." Holding the book in one hand, she planted her other fist on her hip. "Do you hear *me,* Samuel Mast?"

He glowered at her, smoke all but coming out of his ears he was so furious that she was prepared to

defy him. Sarah didn't care. She wasn't going to
give up Ben's book. Not for anyone!

"Is there a problem here?" Ben asked, strolling
out of the dining room. He shot a look toward Samuel, but his obvious concern was for Sarah.

"Everything is fine," she said. Though it wasn't.
How could she possibly marry a man like Samuel
if it meant subverting her own needs and desires?
The same way as she had done as the wife of Amos.

Ben glanced back at Samuel. "Dinner's getting
cold."

Treating Ben as if he weren't there, Samuel said,
"Did the healer give you that book?"

Sarah lifted her chin. "It was a very thoughtful
gift. Helpful, too. I'm sure it will enhance my healing skills—"

"*After* we are married, that woman will not be
welcome in my home. You'll learn your healing
skills from someone else. Or do without." With
that, he marched right between them and into the
dining room.

"What was that all about?" Ben asked, scowling
after the man.

"Nothing." She sighed. Except that she'd given
her word that in little more than a week she'd marry
a man she didn't love. Theirs was almost a business
arrangement, a transfer of farm ownership, a marriage of convenience. A chance for Samuel's children to be raised with a woman in the house who
was unafraid to demonstrate love and affection.

She glanced up at Ben, who was studying her as

he always did, his blue eyes gazing at her so intently that she felt he could read all her doubts.

When she went to her marriage bed with Samuel, she'd give up all hope of ever knowing the caress of a man who loved her, who understood her. As she had done with Amos, she would be forced to do her wifely duty.

But there would be no joy in it for her.

With Ben, she suspected, there would be bliss.

Guilt seared her for even having such a thought, and her face flushed hot. She couldn't sleep with Ben. They couldn't be lovers. Even one night together would be wrong.

But how could she resist, experiencing once that which she would never experience again? Or that which she might have experienced before, six years ago?

Would it be so wrong to give in to this burning desire, so potent it almost took her breath away? She could treat it as an effort to regain her memory through a tactile experience.

But even as she conjured up the excuse, she knew it was a lie.

God help her, she wanted Ben in the same way a budding rose instinctively sought the sun.

Chapter Eleven

From the doorway of the dining room, Sarah asked, "Ben, would you help me?"

"Sure." Muscles aching, he stood and stretched. Harvesting a field of corn was a darn sight harder than he'd realized, and doing it without the help of power equipment ranked right up there among the world's great challenges. "What do you need?"

Fussing with the folds of her apron, Sarah looked nervous. It had been a long day for her, too, feeding a lot of extra mouths and watching out for the younger children, plus putting up with Samuel's constant arrogance. Or maybe it was his own jealousy that was driving Ben crazy.

Fortunately for Ben's sanity, Samuel had taken his family home after dinner. Becky had gone to bed an hour ago, and the house was blessedly quiet. Ben had been thinking about turning in, too, though it had been a relief to sit here I the living room in the comfort of cut-offs and a T-shirt.

"I thought I'd..." A rush of color swept up her

neck and flushed her cheeks. "I thought I'd do some more studying tonight."

She'd been studying here in the living room the past couple of nights. And always on her own. Not understanding what she wanted, he frowned. "And you want me to help you?"

"Yes, please." Her voice was little more than a whisper.

He still didn't get it. "You want me to help you memorize stuff like I used to?"

"Not exactly." Her tongue darted out to moisten her lips. In spite of Ben's fatigue, he felt the gesture way down in his cutoffs. "I thought we could study…in bed."

Now he got it. And it rocked him back on his heels.

"You want to…" His voice cracked.

"Bundle."

That's not exactly what he'd thought she was talking about, or what he'd been hoping for. His teeth clenched, echoing sudden tightness in the rest of his body. "Sarah, honey…"

"If you don't want to, I understand."

"It's not that. Sure I want to. Bundle, I mean. It's just that…" At a loss for words, he crossed the room and slipped his arms around her waist, drawing her close. She smelled of herbs and spices, the sweet scent of woman. "Honey, whenever I touch you—even accidently—I want a whole lot more than just bundling."

"Maybe tonight…if you wanted to cross the

line—'' her whole body trembled as she drew a deep breath, ''—I wouldn't stop you.''

Ben nearly groaned aloud. ''Are you sure, sweetheart?''

''I'm not sure of anything, Ben. There's so much that I've forgotten. There's so much I want to experience.'' The plea in her eyes, the moist threat of tears, was more than any man could refuse. ''Maybe I'm not being fair—''

He didn't give her a chance to finish. Like a starving man, he claimed her mouth, devouring her sweet taste and luscious flavor. He thirsted for her as though he'd traveled a desert for six long, empty years. He'd dreamed of finding her, of discovering her in his arms once more.

Now she would be his again.

Hands shaking with excitement, he slipped the organdy cap from Sarah's head and worked her braid free. Loosening the gossamer strands of flaxen hair, he thread his fingers through the rich thickness and kneaded her scalp. He'd found the oasis that had eluded for him so long.

''Sweet Sarah,'' he murmured.

Caught between the twin prongs of anticipation and fear, Sarah couldn't control the fine tremors that shook her body. She was afraid to think about where this evening would lead, yet even more terrified she'd never have another chance to experience true intimacy with a man who loved her. She wanted to feel cherished, and give back to Ben some small measure of the pleasure she sensed he wanted to give her. To cherish him as well.

With an ease that surprised her, the second fear overwhelmed the first.

"Oh, Ben..." Drawing a shaky breath, she returned his kiss with all the passion that had been lying dormant within her.

She caressed his back, smoothing her hands over his cotton T-shirt, memorizing his sculpted muscles with her fingertips. As he pulled her close, his hips cradled her and she felt the shocking power of his need. And hers.

She gasped in pleasure. Taking his head in her hands, she captured him, drawing him ever closer.

"Sweetheart." He rained kisses on her cheeks and forehead and eyes, making her dizzy with wanting to have his mouth on hers. Their tongues toyed together in a sensuous dance. "I think we'd better take our study session upstairs before things get totally out of hand."

"Yes, please."

Ben took his time as they went upstairs, at each step teasing her with a sensual promise of more to come. A quick nibble on her ear raised goose bumps along her spine. "This kind of homework I've always enjoyed."

"I must have missed this in the books you brought me."

He kissed the sensitive column of her neck, sending heat spiraling to her midsection. "For this home-studying course, I don't need a book."

But she did. She didn't know the rules; they'd been forgotten somewhere in her past. Even so, her body understood its own dictates and responded accordingly. She groaned in pleasure.

He pressed his lips to her hand and moistened her palm with his tongue. "You're definitely an *A* student."

He whispered wicked things in her ear, erotic things that no teacher would ever utter. She thrilled at the forbidden world he described.

Her knees were weak and trembling by the time they reached her bedroom. He closed the door, locking it behind them.

Earlier she had set the lamp on low. The tiny flame flickered, revealing the quilt she'd rolled down the length of the bed. In a gesture of controlled impatience, Ben strode across the room and whipped the bundling barrier away.

"Not this time," he said, his words low and hoarse. "And no clothes. You're so beautiful, I want to see you. All of you."

Deftly he found the pins that held her apron in place. The garments fell away piece by piece, the clothing puddling on the hardwood floor. She shivered as his gaze swept over her in heated approval.

"So very beautiful," he whispered. Bending, he cupped her breast and brushed his lips to the tiny birthmark he had remembered all this time.

She groaned in frustration. Why couldn't she remember *him?*

"Let me see you, too," she pleaded. *Let me remember you.* She'd never seen a naked man that she could recall—not even her husband. With Ben, it seemed as natural as breathing to ask, to know him as intimately as he knew her.

Ben was a work of fine masculine art. His broad shoulders tapered to a narrow waist. His hips were lean, his legs long and muscular. The light arrowing of blond hair on his chest thickened and curled where it formed a nest for his magnificent arousal. For a moment, Sarah was mesmerized by the sheer pleasure of looking at him, and then she blushed hotly at her brazen appraisal.

He seemed not at all bashful as he led her to the bed and lay down beside her. He caressed her slowly, thoroughly, until her breathing became ragged and her heart beat in a jagged rhythm. Like an illusive dream, there was something familiar about the feel of his hands on her. They knew her body more intimately than she knew it herself. Knew how to arouse. When and where to linger. She sensed every part of her recognizing his careful strokes, his gentle caresses, his soft, murmuring words of love.

Every bit of her except her brain remembered him, she thought. She gave a desperate gasp of wanting and frustration.

Even so, in the here and now she relished the newness of this experience, the joy of both past and present coming together in a few glorious moments.

She thrilled at the way he looked at her—his eyes almost indigo—as though he wanted to devour her. His concentration was so intense, she experienced a wondrous sensation. This was not the duty of a marriage bed. With Ben, she felt cherished. Loved.

"Oh, Ben…please," she whispered.

"Easy, love. I want to remember. I want *you* to remember. Everything." Ben angled another kiss across Sarah's lips, recalling in detail the way they molded to his. The giving and taking of their tongues mating together. Her warm, sweet breath exchanging with his. Giving life to his dream.

His hands traveled a journey of rediscovery. Triumph rose within him as he cupped her breast, the shape full and familiar in his palm. He thumbed the nipple, watching it contract—a dusky coral nub he had to taste once again. And he heard a soft sob escape her throat.

So many years, so much loneliness. Finally Sarah was his again.

He reveled in her response to him.

He rained a row of kisses in the valley between her breasts. Sipped from the cup of her belly button. Tested her readiness for him and found her as eager as he. From the very first time, she'd never held back. It wasn't in her nature. And tears burned at the back of Ben's throat that so many years had been wasted.

"I missed you *so* much," he whispered, his voice husky and aching with need.

Sarah's breath tangled in her throat as he rose above her. Her attention splintered. Sensations so pleasurable they were almost painful rippled through her. He was contained power and strength. She savored his mastery of her, and in response she knew the potency of her conquest of him.

She found an ecstasy that she would have

thought impossible. The impact was shattering. Explosive. And as she cried out, his helpless, uncontrollable moans pushed her over the top of some gigantic mountain peak, into oblivion.

They lay panting in each other's arms, his breath hot against her ear, his weight heavy on her. She stroked the breadth of his sweat-dampened back. Tears came to her eyes.

For the life of her, Sarah could not remember ever having felt such deep contentment before.

Nor such despair.

Though she desperately wished it were not so, *she still didn't remember him.*

BEN ROLLED OVER and stretched. He felt about as good as a man could feel. His body hummed as if he'd either had a great workout or...dynamite sex!

His eyes flew open.

He was in Sarah's bedroom, all right, and in her bed, so it hadn't been a dream. He could smell her herbal scent all around him. Still taste her on his lips.

But she was gone. In the early morning light, all that was left of her was the slight indentation of her head on the pillow. Lovingly, he caressed the impression, now cool to his touch.

Damn! He wished she hadn't gotten up so early. He'd gone to sleep holding her in his arms and thinking about how he wanted to make love to her again. As soon as he was able. But he'd been so damn tired. Given the state of his morning arousal, he was more than ready now.

Grinning, he rolled out of bed, found his jeans and pulled them on. He grabbed his T-shirt as he went out the door.

The old rooster out back was announcing dawn as if it were the first time in his life he'd noticed the sun. Ben understood the sentiment. He felt as if last night had been his first time with Sarah all over again.

Barefoot, he padded downstairs. He caught the rich scent of coffee brewing and the yeasty aroma of bread baking. Thoughts of domestic bliss made him feel like the king of the mountain. Pausing at the kitchen door, he drank in the sight of Sarah as she puttered about fixing breakfast. Soon, he promised himself, she'd be in *his* kitchen in that old Victorian house he'd bought just for her, and together they'd be making breakfast—and more babies.

There was something very graceful about the way she moved. Her gestures were sure, her steps confident, her skirt shifting in a subtle, feminine rhythm. Beneath all the yards of fabric that covered her, Ben imagined the supple flow of her muscles, the flex of her soft flesh. His fingers itched with the desire to caress her smooth skin again and feel it heat under his hands.

No woman in the world was more passionate than his Sarah when she was aroused. Absolutely none.

She turned and gasped a little, startled to see him. Her cheeks flushed a pretty shade of pink. "You're not dressed...I mean, dressed like a woman."

"I'm getting pretty darn tired of pretending to be what I'm not."

"But Becky might—"

In a few long strides, he crossed the room and took her in his arms, silencing her with a kiss. For a moment, she held herself rigid, then melted into his embrace. The scent of herbs and yeast and violet soap all mixed together, teasing at his senses.

"You shouldn't do that," she whispered breathlessly when he finally eased up.

"Seemed like a good idea to me," he said with a grin. "In fact, I think I'll do it again."

She planted her palms on his chest and shoved, though not all that hard. "Please, Ben..."

Concerned by her hesitancy, he cocked one brow. "Morning-after regrets?"

"Yes. No. I don't know." Her arms dropped to her sides. "Ben, I've never done anything like that before."

"Yes, you have. I was there, remember?"

"That's the whole point. I *don't* remember. Not you. Not Philadelphia, except in little bits and pieces that don't even seem to fit together. I feel so guilty." A frown stitched itself across her forehead. "I'm sorry."

He pressed a kiss to those furrows. "But you do remember last night, right?"

Nodding, her cheeks colored again.

"We were always that good together, sweetheart. Always."

Beneath her bib apron, her breasts lifted in a sigh. "I'm sure that's true."

"But you don't remember."

"No."

"Well, it doesn't matter. We'll work it out. Unless you get another bash on the head, you'll always remember last night, won't you? I know I will."

To his dismay, tears sprang to her eyes. "Oh, Ben..."

With her tears tearing him up, Ben did what any red-blooded male would do. He kissed her. He couldn't stand that she was so upset, and it scared the heck out of him, for fear her feelings of guilt might frighten her away. He couldn't lose her again. No man was strong enough to endure that kind of loss twice—

"Mama?"

Sarah leapt away from Ben. "Good morning, Becky. Breakfast is almost ready."

Becky tilted her head to one side, studying the pair of them. "Are you Fannie?"

"That's right, Miss Muffet. It's me."

"But you're a *man*," Becky complained.

Sarah groaned.

"'Fraid so," he said, unable to suppress a grin. "Remember, this is how I was dressed when we took you to the hospital that night?"

Her little forehead puckered just like her mother's had a few moments ago. "Is this something else I'm not s'posed to talk about?"

He knelt down to Becky's level. "Think you can keep this big a secret for a while?" At least until he could convince Sarah that the three of them belonged together.

She glanced to her mother for guidance.

"Go wash up, Becky," Sarah said. "Then we'll have breakfast. Hurry, or we'll be late to church."

Backing up a few paces, Becky looked up at Ben. "Does this mean you can really, *really* teach me hammering?"

"You bet it does, munchkin. You'll be the best apprentice carpenter that ever laid a hammer to nails."

With an impish grin, she ran from the room.

As the sound of Becky's footsteps on the stairs subsided, Sarah sighed audibly. Her face had lost all its color and she looked as though she were ready to faint.

"I can't do this, Ben. Not any longer. I can't keep secrets from the people I love."

He wrapped his arms around her. "Fine with me. Let's tell 'em you and I love each other and we're going to be a family—"

"That's not...possible." Her voice trembled. "I made a promise—"

"You made a promise to *me* first. We both made promises to each other a long time ago. I'm trying to keep mine."

For the briefest of moments, she rested her head on his shoulder and then seemed to gather herself. "We have to get ready for church, too."

He wanted to shake her, to *make* her admit there was something special between them, that they did have a future together. But he reined in his impulse, knew this wasn't the time—or the battle—that would win him the war. "How 'bout if I forget my dress and come as a man?"

"You're an outsider. They wouldn't let you past the door."

Ben hugged her tightly, wishing she wouldn't keep slamming the door on him and their past...as well as their future. Last night he'd been so confident he was making progress, that she could and would love him again.

In the bright light of day, he wasn't so sure.

SARAH CLICKED THE REINS and the horse picked up his pace, pulling the buggy into line with the others en route to morning service. Each black buggy maintained the same speed, each family dressed alike, and all the congregants shared the same values. The pressure on individuals to conform to the rules of Amish life was as powerful as flood waters overrunning the banks of a stream after a summer storm. The least violation was detected and eradicated. The bishop saw to that.

She had no idea how she would survive the next three hours. Surely someone would notice that she'd changed, that for the first time within her memory she'd experienced complete and utter satisfaction in a man's arms. And outside the bounds of matrimony, no less. Despite her efforts to contain the feeling, that knowledge must be etched across her face. And glowing in her eyes. How could it not?

Her body still pulsed with new awareness of what Ben had taught her.

Her heart throbbed with the sorrow her transgressions—both past and present—were sure to bring her.

Discovery was imminent now that her daughter knew about Ben. Secrets went into Becky's ears and out her mouth more easily than flour through a sieve. There was no stopping her. Desperately, Sarah wished she'd asked both Ben and Becky to stay at home. Or Ben to leave entirely.

In spite of all the guilt that pummeled her conscience, she could not bring herself to ask Ben to go. Not yet.

But how much longer could his masquerade go undetected even if Becky kept her silence?

When the church elders and congregation learned the truth, what price would Sarah be made to pay? And Becky, too?

Sarah's hands closed more tightly around the reins. "You shouldn't make promises like that."

"Like what?" Ben asked. Sitting next to her, he was now dressed as a proper Amish woman with his cap and long, full dress. But a windowpane would have hidden him better.

Glancing over her shoulder, Sarah made sure that her daughter wasn't eavesdropping on the conversation from the back of the buggy. Whispering, she said, "You told Becky that she can be a carpenter. That's not possible."

"Sure it is, if that's what she wants. I've got women who work on my crews."

"Becky's going to grow up to be an Amish housewife, Ben. She'll bake and sew and do the laundry. Have babies. That's the life she's expected to live.'' One Sarah had been expected to live, too. But she'd failed, slipping from the path her family had intended her to follow. Twice, if she counted last night.

Ben's forehead pinched into a scowl. "She's my daughter, too. As far as I'm concerned, she can be any damn thing she wants. Just like you could be a nurse—or a doctor—if that's what you still want.''

Her heart skipped a beat at the possibility, but an Amish woman gaining a true medical education was no more than a fantasy. "You're giving her false hopes.'' Sarah had learned not to pursue her dreams. For her, it was far too late to even think about such foolishness.

"No, I'm not. Where I come from, women have choices. Maybe it's not easy, and they get harassed on the job, but if she's tough enough and smart enough, Becky can be anything she wants to be, including a contractor. I'd make sure of that.''

How could he possibly promise such pie-in-the-sky dreams to a five-year-old? Failure and disappointment would shatter her hopes. The risk was too great. Better to stay on the sure path among friends and family, rather than striking out on your own.

In spite of the muggy morning, Sarah shivered. She'd tried the other path. She dared not try to escape again.

Nor could she risk losing her child to an outsider. The dilemma tormented her. Search as she might, she had no answer for what the future might hold in store.

THE MEN OF THE congragation in their Sunday-best dark suits and split-tail coats were gathered in animated conversation near the barn. Sarah reined her horse toward an open field where a young man waited to unhitch the buggy for her.

"What's going on?" Ben asked. He reached up to help her down, but Sarah ignored him. It was not seemly for a grown woman to help another unless one was infirm.

"I don't know."

Becky had hopped off the back of the buggy and slipped her hand into Sarah's, then reached for Ben's. "I won't tell," she whispered.

Sarah met Ben's gaze.

He shrugged. "I'm pretty sick of this masquerade anyway."

Suppressing a groan, Sarah led the way to the house where the women were gathered on the porch, as agitated as the men. As they drew closer, she realized they were all assembled around Jenny Beiler.

"Nein, nein," the woman sobbed. "They will not even let me be with my babies alone. Michael must always be there. I can't even bring them home for a visit, for they say I'll hide the children from him."

The women murmured their sympathy, and Sarah's heart lurched. Jenny had lost all three of her babies to a man who was now an outsider.

"Can't someone reason with the sheriff?" asked one of Sarah's neighbors.

"They have tried—" Jenny's voice broke on another sob. "But it does no good. I must leave. I must go with Michael."

To stifle a cry of her own, Sarah's hand flew to her mouth. In desperation, Jenny would walk away from all she had ever known. Her home, her family and friends. To be with her children and to be forever shunned by her own.

It wasn't fair of the church to do that to her, Sarah thought rebelliously. No more so than it was fair for the government to take babies away from their mother.

"What's so bad about her leaving with Michael?" Ben whispered as they stood on the edge of the circle of women. "I thought a wife was supposed to stick with her husband."

"Because her husband is leaving the community, his wife must do the same or lose her children." Sarah shook her head. "That is no choice."

The crowd near the barn began to disperse, and the ordained men of the congregation entered the house by the back door. Momentarily the women hushed.

"They're to decide on the shunning of Hiram King and his family," one of the women whispered.

"What's he done?" Sarah asked in surprise. The family lived a distance from her farm, but she knew them well enough from church services and barn raisings.

"They say he's using an electric milking machine," another woman said, sounding shocked.

The other women present began to buzz their disapproval.

"...It's against the rules..."

"...Flaunting his money, I'd say he was doing..."

"...*Ach, ja,* lording it over the congregation. He always was a braggart, even as a boy..."

"...Too worldly for my taste. You'll see. Unless Hiram gives up his milking machine and asks the elders' forgiveness, the whole family will be shunned..."

Ben took Sarah by the elbow, tugging her away from the crowd of women. Shaken by this latest tragedy, Sarah went with him. Becky escaped her grasp to join Samuel's children in a noisy group of youngsters playing Duck, Duck, Goose on the front lawn. With a practiced mother's eye, Sarah watched to make sure the new arrival was welcomed into the game.

"What's all this fuss about shunning?" he asked when they were clear of the others. It looked as though he'd forgotten or had decided not to wear his false bosom this morning. His chest was broad and flat, and the memory of that wide expanse of masculinity was troubling for Sarah. She kept wanting to lean into him, feel his arms wrapped around her, that masculine chest solid against her breasts.

Forcefully, she set the image aside. "To be shunned is a terrible thing. I don't think I could endure it."

"For using electric milking machines? That's hardly a modern invention."

"It's a *worldly* invention," she insisted. "Using them is enough to have one set apart as an outsider." And surely if the elders knew of her defection from the righteous path, her punishment would be the same...or worse.

"You're too smart to believe using a milking machine is going to send somebody to hell."

"It has nothing to do with being 'smart.' It's what I've been raised to accept. Just because you don't understand our ways doesn't mean they are wrong. Unlike a great many outsiders, our children grow up strong and well-cared for. They respect their elders. Being Amish is not something bad, Benjamin. It's a good life."

Before he had a chance to argue further, they heard the sound of a truck engine. They both glanced toward the lane from the highway to see Seth's Feed Store truck arrive. It was an odd occurrence for Seth to arrive just as church service was to begin, Sarah mused with a prickle of anxiety. Surely the family did not want to take delivery of supplies now.

He parked in front of the house, and a ponderous Amish woman, as broad as she was tall, got out of the truck. She planted herself firmly on the ground, looking around.

"I'm Fannie Raber from Plymouth." Her voice hollered across the farmyard as if she were calling hogs home to supper. "I'm the healer come to teach Forgetful Sarah."

Every eye in the place turned to where Sarah and Ben were standing away from the others—outside the circle of believers.

Fear and shock caught Sarah like a sledgehammer to her midsection, driving the breath from her.

Their ruse had been discovered.

Chapter Twelve

Ben pulled the organdy cap from his head. No sense trying to fool these folks any longer. The couple of hundred people who'd been standing around talking to each other had gone deadly quiet. They looked at him as if he were from outer space.

They knew he was an imposter. They might as well know he was a man.

"Looks like I've been found out," he said under his breath to Sarah, who'd gone as pale as a ghost. "Act surprised and they'll think you didn't know who I was. That I fooled you, too."

Her mouth moved but she didn't speak.

More than anything, Ben wanted her to announce that he was the man she loved—the father of her child—and that the three of them would be leaving as soon as she could get her bags packed. In spite of last night, however, that wasn't going to happen.

God, it hurt!

"The whole of you got lockjaw?" Fannie Raber bellowed into the crowd. "Where is she?"

"I'm Forgetful Sarah." Sarah stepped forward,

her legs unsteady on the uneven grass as she left Ben standing alone. From every direction, eyes bored into her. She had indeed "forgotten" the dreadful feeling of being singled out as a nonconformist. Being tied to a post and whipped until bloody would be no less painful, and over sooner.

"*Ach,* now, that's better." All but shaking the ground with each lumbering step, Fannie marched across the yard. "Seth said you'd likely be at services this morning. They're late starting. What's wrong?"

Sarah swallowed hard, but the ache in her throat didn't go away. "There's been some trouble in the settlement."

"Sickness?"

"*Nein.*" Sarah replied, though she was sick at heart, and the painful knot in her stomach threatened to drive her to her knees. "A family's to be shunned."

And soon she and her daughter would be shunned, too, unless she begged the elders for forgiveness.

Fannie grunted a noncommittal sound. "They said you want to train as a healer."

Once, she'd wanted to be a nurse. The fates intervened. "*Ja, bitte.*"

Ben's hand closed around Sarah's arm. "You could be more than a folk healer, Sarah. Come with me. Please."

From the porch, the woman stared at them, wondering what was happening, no doubt stunned by Ben's unmasking.

Fannie's jowly features pleated into a scowl as her gaze swung to Ben. She perused him top to bottom in disapproval. "Who is this person?"

Tears burned at the back of Sarah's eyes. She didn't know who Ben was. She couldn't remember him. But last night she'd experienced—

"Mama! Mama!" Becky collided with Sarah's thigh and wrapped her arms around her as far as she could reach. "I runned the fastest of *anybody*. Even the boys!"

"Modesty is a virtue you often forget," Sarah said, admonishing her daughter gently in spite of her own roiling emotions.

"Heaven be praised!" the healer cried, her hand covering her ample bosom. "Your daughter is the spittin' image of Amos Yoder's cousin Rachel, thrice removed, when she was a child."

Sarah's jaw dropped. "Becky looks like one of Amos's relatives?" Since Ben had claimed he was Becky's father, Sarah had seen only his image in the child—his eyes, his hair, Becky's shared interest in carpentry.

"*Ach, ja.* Half the Ohio Yoders are blond like her. Here in Peacock they've got the dark hair, but it's the opposite up north. Handsome family, the Yoders are."

Turning quickly, Sarah met Ben's gaze. Perhaps he was wrong. Becky could be Amos's child, after all. But how in heaven's name could she be sure without risking losing her baby? Instinctively she drew Becky more tightly to her.

"Don't believe her," Ben urged, looking stunned.

"Of course she should believe me," Fannie announced loudly, obviously insulted. "Why would I lie about the Yoders, fine people that they are."

"You know the truth," Ben insisted.

Did she? With no memory of their time together, how could Sarah be sure of anything? Even the love he claimed they had once shared.

"*Ach,* the old men are going inside," Fannie said, noting the elders entering the house for worship services. "Seth will take my bags to your house, and I'll go home with you after services."

Numbly, Sarah nodded. "*Ja,* of course. You're welcome to stay."

Sarah felt the congregants' curious interest on both her and Ben as they filed toward the front door, and the newly arrived healer strode out well ahead of them to join the older women at the head of the line. Clearly, no one knew quite what to make of this new revelation—the Fannie they'd already met was not a healer but a man. Sarah wasn't eager to illuminate them. Their unspoken censure was quite enough for now. Later she would no doubt feel the full brunt of their disapproval.

When Sarah reached the front porch, she found Samuel had stepped out of the men's line and was waiting for her and Ben at the bottom of the steps.

"I don't know who you really are," Samuel said, his sun-weathered face darkened with concern and confusion as he stared at Ben. "But you're not welcome here. And you're not welcome anywhere near my wife-to-be." He gave her a curious, almost pained look. "Assuming we are still to be married."

Sarah gasped.

Ben very nearly lost it, then. His fist came up, but before he could deliver a knockout punch, Sarah captured his hand.

"Go, Ben. *Bitte*." Her eyes filled with a desperate appeal for him to do a vanishing act.

He couldn't refuse, not with that much pain and confusion written on her face. He'd never wanted to hurt her. "I'll go—but not very far," he said softly enough that Samuel couldn't hear. "We aren't done yet, Sweet Sarah. Not by a long shot."

With a shake of her head, she turned to go inside. Ben was left standing alone. An *outsider,* as she had always said.

He ripped the bib apron off, letting it drop to the ground. He couldn't give up yet. He'd come so damn close!

INSIDE THE HOUSE, the interior walls were drawn back to allow ample room. Sarah took her seat on a bench on the women's side of the hall. Becky scooted up close to her as though she knew something was terribly wrong.

"Did somebody tell the secret, Mama?" Becky whispered in a childish, too-loud voice. "That Fannie's a *man?*"

Sarah winced and touched her finger to her lips to silence her child. But the damage was done. Condemnation rippled through the room like a snake slithering through tall grass.

On either side of Sarah and Becky, the other women left a wide space in the otherwise crowded room. A feeling of sickness overtook Sarah. Without his cap, they'd seen Ben was a man—a man who'd been living with her these past several weeks.

A man she'd slept with.

Surely they would assume that truth as well. And even if they didn't, it made little difference.

The women knew the discovery of an unrelated man living in her household meant shunning for Sarah…and her daughter. They didn't feel the need to wait for the verdict of the elders. Already they were distancing themselves as a way to protect themselves from contamination. She could hardly blame them. Friendship with her might cost them their families.

Bowing her head, Sarah tried to dredge up a prayer to ask for forgiveness. But all she could see was the hurt in Ben's eyes when she had denied him. *Like Judas.*

A single tear edged down her cheek, and she took Becky's hand in hers as the song leader began the chant for the first hymn. Unless she could redeem herself, she and Becky would be outsiders. Shunned.

And if she did not leave with Ben, she might never again know the love of a man.

Like Jenny who had lost her children, the choice was none at all. To protect her child, to ensure

Becky's future in the safety of the Amish community, Sarah would give up anything the church demanded of her. Including Ben.

Her breath caught on a sob. She could only hope she had the strength to endure the pain. For she loved Benjamin Miller, memories or not. In the here and now, he had stolen her heart.

But in that moment of realization she knew she had to give him up.

For the sake of her child.

BEN WAITED OUTSIDE until he heard the first hymn begin. There wasn't much point in hanging around after that. Sarah wasn't coming back.

Turning, he headed for Seth's truck. Before he got that far, a youngster on crutches came whipping toward him with a speed that only the young can muster. He was the kind of kid who took too many risks and fell off barn roofs.

"Hey, Fannie—"

"Yeah," he responded, the phony name now a part of him.

"I, ah, wanted to thank you." The boy looked at him curiously, not quite sure what to make of Ben.

"No problem."

"The, ah, doctor said you probably saved my life."

Ben cupped the boy's shoulder. "You might think about being a little more careful next time you're up on a roof."

"*Ja,* I will." He flushed and grinned, then sobered to study Ben. "You're not really a healer, are you?"

"Nope. I had a couple of first-aid classes. That's all."

Embarrassed, the boy jammed his hands in his pockets, bunching his jacket around his arms, and studied the tips of his shoes. "Well, ah, I'm glad you were there, anyway. Ma said you've got real good hands."

A carpenter's hands, not a healer's. For Sarah that didn't seem to be enough. "You take care of yourself, son."

In spite of himself, Ben's eyes misted. Damn, he didn't want to give up Sarah or Becky.

A moment later, Ben swung up into the passenger seat of Seth's truck. "Thanks for waiting."

"Sorry I couldn't let you know the real Fannie was coming. That's the disadvantage of not having a phone."

Ben shrugged.

"I figured you'd need a ride into town."

"No, take me to Sarah's."

"To get your stuff?"

"She and I still have some talking to do." He'd come this far. He planned to give it one more shot.

He didn't want the new healer to be a part of his conversation with Sarah, so he intended to wait in the barn. Sooner or later she'd have to put the horse away. Then they could talk alone.

As Seth started the truck, the engine drowned out the sound of the Amish chanting their morning hymns—part of a world in which Ben would find neither welcome nor comfort.

THE KITTENS WERE in a playful mood. Ben gently wrestled with them, ignoring the prick of their tiny teeth when they bit down on his hand. The pain he was feeling went a lot deeper than that.

As a kid he'd wondered what he'd done so wrong that he didn't deserve a decent family. He still hadn't figured out the answer.

The wait seemed like an eternity, but he finally heard the soft *whir* of the buggy wheels and the steady beat of the horse's hooves returning to the farm. Fannie Raber shouted some words of praise about Sarah's garden, and then they went inside the house.

Dust motes danced in the column of sunlight that slanted in the open barn door, and the heat inside rose by several degrees. The scent of hay hung heavily in the warm air. Sweat sheened Ben's face and was edging down his spine by the time Sarah walked her horse and buggy into the barn.

"Let me help you," he said.

She squealed in surprise, her heart nearly leaping into her throat. "What are you doing here? I thought you'd left."

The horse jerked his head, and Ben grabbed the bridle she'd let go.

"I want you and Becky to come with me, Sarah. Back to Philadelphia."

Dear heaven, he didn't know what he was asking of her, or how badly she was tempted. But her child's future was at stake, as was her own. "I can't, Ben."

"Why not? You know I love you. Becky, too."

"In spite of what you think, she might not be your child. The healer said—"

"I don't give a flying fig what that old battle-ax says. And it doesn't matter if I'm Becky's biological father or not. I love her like she was my own kid. I want us to be a family."

Sarah didn't doubt his feelings for Becky. Or for her. But she felt trapped by her past, by her Amish roots and beliefs. Her two lives existed at the opposite end of a spectrum. She couldn't seem to find a way to cross over to Ben while still meeting her other obligations.

When she didn't respond, he unhooked the harness and led the horse into his stall, patting the gelding on the rump with a big, gentle hand.

"Ben, have you ever thought about... You could convert, Ben. Become Amish. The farm is mine. We could live here—"

"I can't hide out from the world like you people do. Life isn't easy on the outside, but it's real. You used to think you could make it out there. With me. What have they done to you to make you so damn scared of your own shadow?"

"It's not like that. I'm not scared." But she was. Terrified and confused over what she could not remember. "I have responsibilities here, particularly to Becky. I can't walk away from all that." The outside world Ben spoke of so glibly was totally foreign to her, and therefore frightening. Being rebellious at eighteen was one thing. Now she was old enough, mature enough, to realize there were no easy answers in life. Bad things *did* happen, even to good people, and she had her daughter to protect.

"I can take care of Becky and you, too. I've got money now, Sarah. Plenty of it. I bought an old Victorian house. For you, Sarah, not for myself. I always hoped I'd find you someday. It's got six bedrooms—enough for all the kids you ever wanted—and an acre of ground. You can grow vegetables and herbs, whatever you want."

"You're asking too much of me, Ben. Maybe as an eighteen-year-old I had enough courage to leave the settlement—or maybe I was just plain foolish."

"Or maybe you came back because I don't deserve you. That I'm not good enough to be loved by anybody."

"Oh, no, that's not true!" Unable to stand the pain and hurt she saw in his eyes, Sarah went to him. She couldn't let him go like this, when she'd been the cause of his suffering.

And, if she allowed herself to admit the truth, she wanted the feel of Ben's mouth on hers, his arms around her, one more time before she was forced to close the door on her secret dreams. The elders were coming that afternoon. To keep her place in the community—to avoid shunning—they would demand she repent for *all* her sins. One more transgression wouldn't change the outcome.

"If it's not true, then why can't I have you?" With a growl of frustration, Ben pulled Sarah to him. He claimed her mouth with a fierce, possessive kiss. He plunged his tongue into her sweet flavor and ground his lips into hers.

On the inside he was dying, but his body pulsed with need. It was like a beast that wouldn't let go. For six years he'd thought of her every day, missed her every hour. Wasn't that enough penance for whatever awful crime he'd committed as a kid? For not having been good enough to be loved?

He wanted to strip her bare and take her right there in the barn in a bed of fresh-smelling hay. He wanted to drive himself into her and feel her legs lock around his waist. He wanted to hear her soft cries when her pleasure peaked. He never wanted to let her go.

But it was her choice, not his. She had to *want* to come to him.

"Sarah, sweetheart—" His breathing broke on a jagged intake of air.

"Ben...I'm so sorry."

This was tearing her apart. He couldn't stand to see her so tormented, hadn't known how hard it would be to leave her once he'd found her again. But he couldn't make her suffer anymore. He dug deep in his gut for a love strong enough to let her go.

"I'm going to send you the keys to my bike. I'll have Seth bring it around and put it in Hosettler's barn with John's car. If you ever change your mind—*ever*—all you and Becky have to do is come to me in Philadelphia. Seth will know where I am."

"I can't drive a motorcycle," she protested. "How could I—"

"I taught you, Sarah. We were out practicing when you hit a patch of ice. The bike got away from you and we slid into a lamppost."

"I caused the accident?" she gasped.

"The ice did, honey. You were doing fine till then." He took her face between his hands and kissed her again. Softly. With all the longing he felt. When he tasted salty tears, he didn't know if they were his or hers. "Now I'm going to tell Becky goodbye, then I'll hitch a ride into town."

"Ben, I can't think—"

"You do what you think is right, Sarah. For you and our daughter. Whatever you choose—"

He couldn't go on. There weren't any words strong enough, powerful enough to convince Sarah that he was right. He couldn't argue with what she believed, even if she was dead wrong to be afraid to come with him. She'd have to figure it out for herself.

He hoped he'd see her again. But he would never, ever come back to Peacock.

"Don't forget me this time, Sweet Sarah. I love you."

Chapter Thirteen

The imaginary roar of a motorcycle filled her head as Sarah watched Ben kneel beside the porch steps to talk to Becky. His jeans pulled taut across his buttocks in the same way the denim fabric would if he were riding his bike. His loose hair hanging to his shoulders gave him a touch of wildness. But the gentle way he took Becky in his arms and hugged her nearly broke Sarah's heart.

She rubbed at her temple as the throbbing rose to a crescendo. She'd come close to killing both herself and Ben on that motorcycle. In spite of what he'd said, she knew her inexperience had been to blame. She should be asking his forgiveness—because of the accident. Because she'd forgotten him.

Instead she was sending him away.

Dear heaven, without her memory of their time together, how could she know what was right for her child? Or even for herself?

All her life she'd be taught duty came first—to her family, community and faith. How could she change that now? If in the past she'd rebelled, she'd obviously failed. Now it seemed too risky.

Yet only Ben has the power to make my heart sing.

She stayed in the shadow of the barn until Ben stood and walked alone down the lane toward the highway. A part of her wanted to run after him— the part that remembered her youthful rebellion. Among the Amish, discipline was far more important than demonstrating affection. As a child, she'd longed to be held on her father's lap and hugged. Instead, she'd more often been severely scolded for small infractions.

Just as Amos had reprimanded Becky for the slightest misdeed. Even when the child had been too young to understand what she'd done wrong.

In contrast, Ben gave his affection easily, not only to her and Becky but to others in the community. Yet he didn't believe he deserved love in return.

Heaven help her! She had fallen in love with him, perhaps for the second time. But rather than telling him how she felt—rather than upsetting the status quo—she'd sent him away.

And now, in her confusion, she didn't want him to go.

"Mama, how come Fannie has to go away?" Becky looked up at her with big blue eyes, so much like Ben's that it made Sarah's heart lurch. Yet it was also possible those eyes and her daughter's fair coloring came from the Yoder side of the family.

Which was the truth? And did Sarah even want to know? What earthly good would it do her?

I love her like she was my own kid, he'd said.

Automatically, she cupped Becky's head and pulled her tightly against her thigh. "He's an outsider, my little munchkin," she said, using one of Ben's endearments.

"I thought 'cause he's a man he could be my new papa."

Sarah shook her head. "Samuel will be your papa soon." And raise her in the Amish way. As Sarah had been raised.

"I wish it could be Fannie, Mama."

"*Ja,* I know. His real name is Ben—Benjamin Miller." *He might be your real father.*

"Ben." The child seemed to taste the word, then gave an approving nod. "Ben said we could come see him if we want."

Her throat tightened. "I don't think so." Sarah didn't know how to drive a motorcycle. Not anymore. She only knew how to be a good Amish wife who obeyed her husband and did her duty by him. That's what the past six years—and all of the life that she could remember—had taught her.

Other lessons she might have learned had been lost, along with her memory of Ben.

As the real Fannie Raber came out the front door, Sarah tried to concentrate on her future as a helper in the community and the mother of Samuel's children. She felt little joy at the prospect. Only a sense of obligation.

"Come now, Forgetful Sarah," Fannie shouted. "We've work to do."

With Becky lingering nearby as though she were afraid her mother might leave the way Ben had, Sarah examined the healer's collection of herbs arranged in neatly labeled jelly jars. The threat of tears made the letters blur. Concentration was impossible, and Fannie's overly loud instructions were like the pounding of a carpenter's hammer inside Sarah's skull.

Ben was a carpenter and more. Dear God, she missed him already.

At mid-afternoon Samuel arrived, asking to speak with her alone. He stood tall and erect in his black Sunday suit, his wide-brim hat squarely on his head even though he was in her living room.

"This person we knew as Fannie is gone?" he asked.

Head bowed, she swallowed hard. *"Ja."* Gone but not forgotten. Not this time.

"I've talked with the bishop and elders."

Sarah nodded. She'd been braced for a confrontation with the entire leadership of the church. Apparently they had decided her being chastised by Samuel, the person most injured by her actions, would be enough. For now.

"My children need a mother, and I need a wife to tend them."

"I know." A month ago the prospect of being a mother to Samuel's children had been a happy one. Now it seemed only a duty.

"I am willing to forget the past and forgive you, if that is your wish."

She lifted her chin and met his gaze levelly. "Are you willing to love me?"

A flush stole slowly into his cheeks, deepening his complexion to a ruddy, sun-baked brown. "I intend to do my husbandly duty by you and respect you as a woman, if that is what you are asking."

No, that wasn't the question her heart wanted answered.

"The elders wanted to delay our wedding. I argued against it."

"Does that mean you care for me?"

He looked surprised. "Of course I do. But I have no need for a wife who is shunned."

"My choice is to marry you or be shunned?"

"It is a reasonable choice."

For him, maybe. "And Becky? She would be shunned, too?"

"Unless she lives with an Amish family and has no contact with you."

Sarah sucked in a quick breath. The threat Samuel and the elders were making was as horrifying as that of Jenny's husband. Sarah would give up her own life first before giving away her child. To anyone.

It is no choice at all.

"I will marry you, Samuel Mast, and do my duty as I have vowed. For the sake of my child."

With a nod, he visibly relaxed his taut shoulders. Samuel was not a bad man, Sarah knew. But neither

would she be able to love him as she loved Ben—
the man she had sent away.

FOR THE NEXT three days, Sarah's head spun with
new information about using mullein oil, garlic and
catnip, among a hundred other herbs and curatives.
Fannie adjusted Sarah's spine to improve her som-
ber mood, but had only limited success. In return,
Sarah practiced the technique on the healer, whose
spirits never seemed to flag.

At night Sarah lay in her lonely bed, reading the
medical guide Ben had given her until her eyes
burned with fatigue. But she couldn't sleep, at least
not soundly. Instead she dreamed of him, of Ben's
kisses and the way he held and caressed her. Loved
her. She woke in the mornings with the flowered
silk scarf clasped in her fist, and used it to wipe the
tears from her cheeks.

The thought of leaving her home and all that was
familiar to her to go in search of Ben left her par-
alyzed with fear. Her dreams, when they weren't
filled with Ben, were haunted by that gang of cutthroats who had once accosted her, and the censur-
ing looks of her parents the morning she'd awakened in the hospital.

LESS THAN A WEEK after Ben left, Becky started
school. It was a milestone Sarah dreaded, though in
truth she could have had Becky wait another year
before attending the one-room schoolhouse. But her
child was simply too advanced to wait. Finally,

after lengthy discussion, the Amish teacher had agreed.

Sarah's child was no longer a baby and her arms ached to hold another infant to her breast. *Ben's child.*

Given the agreement she'd made with Samuel, she dared not think like that.

Eager to hear news of the first day of school, Sarah walked down the lane to meet her daughter that afternoon. A touch of autumn chilled the air, and she inhaled deeply, catching the faint scent of burning leaves. Where was Ben now? she wondered. And had he left his motorcycle in Hosettler's barn as he had promised?

She glanced longingly in that direction. The power lines that crossed the road to the neighbor's house reminded Sarah that they were outsiders. *As is Ben.*

If only he had been willing to convert—

"Mama! Mama!"

Turning, Sarah smiled as Becky ran toward her, and her heart filled with love. Surely she was doing the right thing for her daughter's future by staying within the safety of the Amish community. Here they had no gangs or drugs. Children, even though they might chafe at the rules during adolescence, respected their elders. The horrors that plagued big cities did not touch Amish lives. Their very "difference" protected them from worldly influences.

Unless, of course, they went "outside," as Sarah had, to pursue a worldly dream. Invariably, the experience shook the foundation of their beliefs. But Sarah had forgotten—

"Mama! Mama! The teacher made me miss recess." Becky flew into Sarah's arms, her face streaked with tears.

Frowning, Sarah knelt and caught her child. "You were made to stay in on your first day of school? Why?"

"She said Josh was the best 'scholar' of all us new students." She sniffed and swallowed a sob. "And I said it wasn't so."

"You shouldn't have corrected the teacher."

"But she was wrong!" Becky wailed. "I was best! I know all my numbers and letters. I can even *read!*"

"Maybe Josh was trying very hard. That counts, too."

"She told me I had to help Josh, but he stuck his tongue out at me when the teacher wasn't looking."

"Oh, my..."

"So I punched him. But not very hard," she hastily added.

"Becky, you know I don't approve of fighting."

"But you want me to be smart, don't you?"

"Of course I want you to be smart," Sarah answered. What mother wouldn't value her child's intelligence? But being "smart" was not particularly valued among the Amish. More important was working cooperatively with your neighbors, or having the talent for planting and harvesting. As a girl,

Becky had little chance of receiving praise for that particular skill. That was the Amish way.

"From now on, Becky, you must try to *help* other children, not brag that you are smarter than they are."

Her expression crumbled in dejection. Her chin dropped to her chest. "*Ja*, Mama," she whispered, her eyes filling with a new load of tears and her chin quivering. She shuffled away from Sarah, her youthful spirit broken.

Just as Sarah's had been broken by the same strictures that limited a woman's future. A knot twisted in her stomach. By staying here and marrying Samuel, was she *betraying* her own daughter?

In time, would her child rebel and leave the community, just as Sarah had done years ago?

Before she followed Becky down the lane to the house, she checked her mailbox at the edge of the road. The weekly Amish newspaper had arrived along with a letter, her address scrawled in an unfamiliar hand.

She ripped open the envelope, and her breath caught as a key slid into her palm. A motorcycle ignition key. With her hands trembling, she unfolded a single sheet of paper. A map to Philadelphia. To Ben's house. The distance was no more than fifty miles, an easy journey on a motorcycle.

"Oh, Ben." Confusion and indecision twisted within her like a dust devil racing across a newly plowed field. Somehow she had to find the wisdom of Solomon—and she had to find it soon.

Come this Sunday and her marriage to Samuel, her fate and that of her daughter would be sealed.

FROM THE TWENTIETH FLOOR of a high-rise under construction, Ben looked out over the Philadelphia skyline. There weren't any solid walls to break his view. But between him and Sarah, the vast barrier of fear and tradition seemed insurmountable.

Once he'd admired her for having more courage than men who walked the high steel girders without a safety line. He could only hope she'd find that reservoir of fearlessness again, and come to him.

Mac Culdane, his partner, worked his way across the girder. "Glad you're back, Ben. The suppliers have been giving me fits with their damn late deliveries. You need to apply a little of your charm to get things moving."

His lips twitched but he couldn't quite bring himself to smile. Maybe he ought to put on his Amish costume and "charm" them as a woman. "I'll talk to 'em." In the past, getting the job done, building bigger and better skyscrapers, had seemed important. He'd wanted to impress Sarah once he found her again.

Now it didn't seem to matter.

Mac rested his hand on Ben's shoulder. "Looks like that vacation you took didn't do you much good. You okay?"

"I'm fine."

"What you need is a good woman, Ben. My ole lady has a niece—"

"No." Stepping past his partner, Ben headed for

the cage-like construction elevator. There was only one woman he needed. Either she'd come or she wouldn't. He'd done all he could.

And if she didn't show up by Sunday, he was damn well going to tie on the biggest drunk anyone had ever seen.

Even then, he'd never be able to forget Sarah.

"THEY SAY, ON THE OUTSIDE, brides always wear white." Short Martha, whom Sarah had asked to be her wedding attendant, fussed with Sarah's plain navy bib apron, smoothing the fabric across her shoulders. They were waiting for the ceremony to begin in the back room of the house where the wedding would take place during a regular Sunday service.

"I suspect Samuel would find white far too impractical. At the very least, he'd expect me to scrub the floors in it tomorrow."

Martha chuckled, but Sarah did not. Her nerves were pulled as taut as the fabric on a quilting frame. At the merest hint that her decision to marry Samuel was wrong, she was ready to flee. Alternatively, she'd prayed for a fire to break out in the barn or a tornado to appear on the horizon. *Please, God, give me a sign.*

Martha straightened her cap and pulled the strings evenly under Sarah's chin. "I had thought you might be marrying an outsider by now—not Samuel."

Sarah frowned, her stomach tripping over the possibility. "Why do you say that?"

"When I met the *first* Fannie, I suspected he had come—"

"You knew he was a man?"

"That night of the quilting bee. Others only saw what they expected to see in the healer, but from where I sat, it was obvious that he was a man. And very handsome, too."

"How did you know so quickly, for heaven's sake? He fooled me." At least at first, though she had felt *something* even from the beginning. A sexual spark that she hadn't been able to explain until much later. A feeling she had never experienced with any other man. And didn't expect to discover with Samuel.

"He sat with his knees spread wide apart like he was straddling a horse," Martha said with a smug grin. "Amish women never do that. And when he looked at you…" She shrugged her hunched shoulders. "It was the way a man looks at the woman he loves."

"If you knew he was a man right off, why didn't you tell me?"

"I had the feeling you had known him while you were away. During your forgotten time. If so, then he must have loved you very much to have searched for you so long and to have disguised himself so thoroughly. Or tried to. It seemed possible you might change your mind about marrying Samuel. I had hoped you would."

Astounded, Sarah stared at her friend. "You mean, you wanted me to—"

"Samuel and I have been friends for as long as

I can remember. But he has never looked at me as a woman, though who can blame him since I hardly come up past his waist.'' She tried to laugh, but this time it was less convincing. ''When he married Tillie, I understood. She was a wonderful girl. But when she passed on, I had hoped…I know it was wicked of me.''

''My merciful heavens! You love him, don't you?'' Martha loved Samuel's children, too. Sarah had seen her friend playing with them, kissing them, being the attentive cousin. But it was an act. She loved them as a mother would.

''It doesn't matter. You'll be a good wife to him, and we'll all still be friends.'' Martha's sweet smile nearly broke Sarah's heart.

''But that's not fair. You should be able to marry the man you love.'' *And so should I,* she realized. What truly was holding her here in Peacock? Only a sense of obligation and her own fears of the unknown. She was no longer close to her parents. The tension since her accident—and her subsequent marriage—was too great a barrier to easily bridge. And while she felt great loyalty to the community, did they not owe her something in return?

If she married Samuel, she risked destroying her daughter's dreams and stealing from Martha the man she loved.

Suddenly Sarah knew. The price was far too high to pay. She needed to follow her heart.

Grabbing Martha's hand, she dragged her friend out a back door and around to the front of the house.

"What are you doing, Sarah?" Martha objected. With her short legs, she had to hurry to keep up.

"I just got the sign I was looking for. I'm doing something about it."

The ordained men of the congregation were beginning to file into the house, the eldest leading the way. Sarah barreled through the crowd of stern-faced men until she found Samuel.

"We have to talk," she announced breathlessly.

His gaze darted from Sarah to Martha and back again. "What is all this? We are to be—"

"It's a mistake, Samuel. I thought I could go through with the ceremony, but it's not right. I don't love you. Short Martha does."

Her announcement was like a blanket smothering a fire. The oxygen vanished from the air. The men who were moving into the house, their expressions puzzled, gave them a wide berth. In the yard, only the sound of horses grazing in the pasture disturbed the silence.

"Is that true, Martha?" Samuel asked, his dark eyes softening.

She didn't meet his gaze. "You deserve a woman who can give you children. The doctor—"

"Do you love me?" he persisted, kneeling to be closer to her height.

When their eyes finally met, it was the sweetest sight Sarah had ever seen. They were two lovers who had never realized the possibilities.

Neither had she, until now. She could only hope it wasn't too late.

Assuming Samuel and Martha would find a way

to explain the change in plans to the congregation—
and to find their own happiness—she slipped away
from the couple and went in search of Becky. Hush-
ing the child's questions, she ushered her out of the
house and to their waiting buggy. She needed to
pack a few things and arrange for the chickens to
be fed and the horse to be cared for.

Then she would be on her way to Philadelphia.
And Ben.

Her hand closed around the talisman key hidden
deep in the pocket of her skirt. *Please, Ben, don't
give up on us yet.*

BECKY'S EYES OPENED so wide they nearly popped
out of her head at the sight of Ben's motorcycle.
"We're gonna ride that?"

"That's the plan," Sarah told her daughter,
though her level of confidence wasn't all that high.

"Do you know how?"

"Ben taught me." He'd taught her how to love,
too. Twice. She had to have faith she'd remember
this skill, too, once the time came.

"Will he teach me, too?" Becky was so excited
about Ben being her father that she was bursting
with it.

"When you're older, munchkin. *Much* older."

Undaunted, Becky raced circles around the
motorcycle, her Amish costume in striking contrast
to the red helmet Ben had left behind for his daughter. "He's going be the best papa ever, isn't he,
Mama?"

"*Ja,* I think so."

Hiking up her skirt, she straddled the bike and pulled on her own helmet. Her fears tangled in her throat as she helped Becky settle on the seat behind her. "Hold on tight," she urged her daughter.

Dear heaven, what if she crashed again? What if she killed her own child?

Taking a deep breath, she fisted her hands around the black grips and closed her eyes. The image of a ribbon of asphalt speeding past her popped into her mind, and she heard Ben's voice as clearly as if he were riding behind her. *Remember, the right hand is the throttle, the left is your clutch. Twist slowly. You don't have to go fast.*

All his instructions came back to her in a rush. How to lean into the curves. When to let up on the accelerator. The way she should finesse the gears with a light touch of her toe. She grinned and tightened her helmet strap under her chin.

In her mind's eye she could see the apartment where they'd lived together—the flowered curtains, potted plants on the windowsill, the mussed sheets on the bed after they'd made love. Memories swirled, making her nearly giddy with hope. All the love she'd felt for him—then and now—filled her with joy.

She belonged with Ben and so did their daughter.

BEN POPPED THE TOP on his second can of beer. The first one hadn't tasted all that good. But he was determined to get smashed.

Sunday night. She wasn't coming.

He walked across the living room of the old Victorian house. He'd refinished the hardwood floor, and it shone like new, but there were only a couple of pieces of furniture in the room. He'd figured Sarah would want to decorate the place.

What a stupid jerk he'd been to dream he could have a decent family. He ought to sell the place and go back to his old apartment. But there'd be too many memories there.

Downing a swig of beer, he let the bitter taste burn at the back of his throat. Somebody was making a ruckus outside, revving an engine. Hell, he wanted a little peace and quiet so he could wallow in his misery.

Looking for a fight, he yanked open the front door and stalked outside. The house stood well back from the street and none of the streetlights reached quite this far. He could barely make out the figure on a motorcycle. It was probably a juvenile delinquent who thought the place would be a good target to vandalize.

Just let him try, Ben thought grimly. He'd like nothing better than to get in a fight tonight. A perfect way to celebrate Sarah's wedding to another man.

The bike coasted to a stop right in front of him. The driver looked like a teenager—slender shoulders and not very tall. The kid on the back was no bigger than a midget. He was gonna clean their clocks!

"I wasn't sure this was the right house."

Everything slid into slow motion and Ben went

very still. He must have had more to drink than he realized. This had to be a dream.

"Sar-ah?" His voice cracked. He didn't want to wake up.

Becky hopped off the bike and came running toward him, her skirts flying as she tossed aside her helmet. "Ben! Ben! We're here and you get to be my new papa!"

The air whooshed out of his lungs as the child launched herself at him. He squeezed her tightly. This was no dream. She was flesh and blood. So was Sarah.

He hitched Becky onto his hip, walking the rest of the way down the brick path to the driveway. He could hardly believe his eyes as Sarah removed her helmet and set it on the bike.

She'd come to him.

Just to make sure he wasn't still dreaming, he cupped her face with his free hand. Warm, soft flesh like peaches and cream.

She smiled tentatively. "I'm sorry, Ben, that it took me so long to remember. I got lost getting here, and I was afraid to drive too fast."

"It doesn't matter." His throat felt as raw as if he had swallowed a handful of razor blades. "You're here now."

"I love you, Benjamin Miller." She glanced at their daughter, who was locked on Ben's hip. "We both do. We'd like to be your family, if you'll have us."

He couldn't speak. There weren't any words in the entire world strong enough to express how he felt. An incredible weight had been lifted from his shoulders. *His family.*

Drawing Sarah to him, he kissed her with all the pent-up emotion he felt, trying to let her feel how much he cherished her. Sarah's lips molded to his, a perfect match.

Becky tugged on Ben's shirt. "Am I not s'posed to tell about you kissin' Mama?"

Ben laughed, a low rumbling sound that felt as if it came from deep in his heart. "Little Miss Muffet, you can tell the whole world about me kissing your mom, 'cause I plan to do it again every chance I get."

Gathering his family into a three-way hug, Ben knew he'd never known such happiness as he did this very minute. He expected the feeling would last a lifetime.

Epilogue

One year later

Nine-pound, six-ounce Culdane Miller—named for Ben's partner—lay nestled in Sarah's arms. Ben leaned over the bed railing to kiss Sarah, thinking she had to be the most beautiful new mom in the entire world. He figured young Dane thought so, too, from the contented look on his face. He was so proud of his son, his whole family, he'd strung a banner from the top of the just-completed Philadelphia Towers. He wanted everyone to know how lucky he was.

"How're you feeling?" Ben asked Sarah as his fingers caressed the downy top of Dane's head.

She gave him one of her angelic smiles, then looked at their son. "Never better."

"I'm not sure I want to go through that ordeal again anytime soon. I wasn't sure I was going to make it."

"You?" She raised her brows. "I thought I was the one doing all the work."

"Not a chance, Sweet Sarah. I'd go through a molten river of fire before I put you through that much agony again."

Taking his hand, she kissed his palm and brought it to her cheek. "It was worth every minute, sweetheart. Just look at him...and our beautiful daughter." She smiled at Becky, who was tight up against Ben's side. "You want to see your little brother, *ja?*"

Becky nodded, though she looked more hesitant than excited.

Ben hefted her up. "Easy now. Don't jiggle the bed. Your mom's still kinda hurting."

For a long moment, Becky just looked at the baby.

"What's wrong, Miss Muffet?" Ben asked. "Don't you like Dane?"

"I guess." She sighed, long and expressively. "But he's gotta grow a *whole* lot before I can teach him to hammer."

Ben laughed and gave her a big squeeze, then tugged a couple of sheets of paper from his hip pocket. "Your biology teacher was scared to death when you went into labor during the midterm."

"Well, I couldn't very well leave, could I? I mean..." Frowning, she eyed the papers in his hand. One of the first things Ben had done after their marriage was encourage her to enroll in school again. She'd been proud as a peacock to sign up for classes as Sarah Miller. "Is that the test back already?"

"Yep." Bursting with as much pride as if it were

his own exam results, Ben handed her the test. "A perfect score."

"On all counts," she said and sighed, rising up with the help of the bed rail to envelop Ben, Becky and tiny Culdane in a hug. "I must be the luckiest woman in the world."

Ben could only speak for himself. And he knew *he* was the happiest man this side of heaven.

"I got ahold of your mom," he said. "She said she loved you and would get here to see you and the baby—come hell or high water."

Sarah's eyes widened. "My mother said *that?*"

"An exact quote." He grinned. "And I think she's working on your dad. I figure I need to get the guest room ready."

Tears of happiness filled her eyes. "Thank you, Benjamin. I love you so much...."

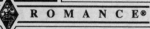
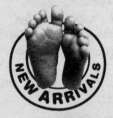

Three compelling novels
by award-winning writer

KAREN YOUNG
HEAT of the NIGHT

**Three dramatic stories of the risks men and
women take to protect their children.**

Debt of Love—Tyler Madison and Alexandra Tate are
drawn together by the urgent need to help Tyler's nephew
after a devastating accident.

Touch the Dawn—Mitchell St. Cyr flees with his children
to protect them from their stepfather and finds haven with
his friends until he learns that their daughter Jacky is a
county juvenile officer.

The Silence of Midnight—When his son is kidnapped,
Sheriff Jake McAdam feels he's failed—as a lawman, a
husband, *a father.*

On sale December 1999 at your favorite retail outlet.

HARLEQUIN®
Makes any time special ™

Visit us at www.romance.net

PSBR3100

**Starting December 1999,
a brand-new series about
fatherhood from**

Three charming stories
about dads and kids...
and the women who
make their families
complete!

Available December 1999
FAMILY TO BE (#805)
by Linda Cajio

Available January 2000
A PREGNANCY AND A PROPOSAL (#809)
by Mindy Neff

Available February 2000
FOUR REASONS FOR FATHERHOOD (#813)
by Muriel Jensen

Available at your favorite retail outlet.

Come escape with Harlequin's new

Series Sampler

**Four great full-length Harlequin novels
bound together in one fabulous volume
and at an unbelievable price.**

Be transported back
in time with a
Harlequin Historical®
novel, get caught up
in a mystery with Intrigue®,
be tempted by a hot, sizzling romance
with Harlequin Temptation®,
or just enjoy a down-home
all-American read with
American Romance®.

You won't be able to put this collection down!

On sale February 2000 at your favorite retail outlet.